A Candlelight
Ecstasy Romance®

"I DON'T WANT THAT TO HAPPEN AGAIN, AUTUMN!"

"It was only a ki—"

"I *know* what it was!" His grip on her arm tightened. "And I don't want you to do it again."

"Don't be so self-righteous, Cade. It was just a kiss and I did have your complete cooperation, didn't I?"

"Your veneer of sophistication doesn't mean you've grown up. You're still a child, running home to bandage a broken heart, and I'm not going to play nursemaid this time. Be careful, Autumn, about backing our friendship into a corner!" He released her and stepped away.

But now it was her turn to stop him. Her fingers closed on his muscular forearm. "And *you* be careful, Cade, of thinking I'm still a child. No matter how you feel, sooner or later you'll have to accept the fact that I've grown up . . . and I have, Cade, I have."

A CANDLELIGHT ECSTASY ROMANCE®

EVER A SONG

Karen Whittenburg

A CANDLELIGHT ECSTASY ROMANCE®

Published by
Dell Publishing Co., Inc.
1 Dag Hammarskjold Plaza
New York, New York 10017

Dell ® TM 681510, Dell Publishing Co., Inc.

Candlelight Ecstasy Romance®, 1,203,540, is a registered
trademark of Dell Publishing Co., Inc.,
New York, New York.

ISBN: 0-440-12389-5

Printed in the United States of America
First printing—November 1984

*In memory of Marisa,
who taught me many things about
friendship.*

To Our Readers:

We have been delighted with your enthusiastic response to Candlelight Ecstasy Romances®, and we thank you for the interest you have shown in this exciting series.

In the upcoming months we will continue to present the distinctive, sensuous love stories you have come to expect only from Ecstasy. We look forward to bringing you many more books from your favorite authors and also, the very finest work from new authors of contemporary romantic fiction.

As always, we are striving to present the unique, absorbing love stories that you enjoy most—books that are more than ordinary romance.

Your suggestions and comments are always welcome. Please write to us at the address below.

Sincerely,

The Editors
Candlelight Romances
1 Dag Hammarskjold Plaza
New York, New York 10017

CHAPTER ONE

She knew he would be there. Long before she reached the end of the familiar path, Autumn heard the sound of his soft melodious whistle. Of course Cade would be at the boat dock. Where else would he be on her first day back?

He could have been at the marina. Or at the store. He could have been sailing the blue-gray waters of Chesapeake Bay, but she had known with the intuition of long-standing friendship that he would be here.

Quiet pleasure stirred inside her and her smile began even before the boat house came into full view. The weathered shingles on the rooftop were as colorless as the clapboard siding, but Autumn felt a reminiscent contentment surround her. For as long as she could remember, the boat house had stood just so . . . a patient, friendly sentinel between her home and Cade's. Technically, she supposed, it belonged to the O'Connors, but she had claimed it for the Tremaynes when she was six years old and no one had ever questioned her right to be there.

Autumn stopped to dwell on the familiar scene and the childhood memories that echoed with laughter, her laughter and Cade's. It had been so long since she'd seen him and until now she hadn't realized how much she'd missed him. Much more than she'd missed her brother, Ross, and his family. Even more than she'd missed the peaceful solitude of this quiet corner of the world.

And she'd never expected to miss any of it. Her lips completed the smile. It was, at last, good to be home.

The low whistle came again, tugging her forward, teasing her with its indiscernible tune. With a tingle of anticipation Autumn walked to the wooden dock, then hesitated, one foot on the grass, one foot on a redwood slat. Cade was on the sailboat polishing the curved railing of the bow and unaware of her presence.

Knees bent, faded cutoffs stretched tight across muscled legs and hips, without a' shirt or hat, he concentrated on the task. His shoulders were tanned and broad and his arms flexed with subtle strength. His skin glistened bronze in the sunlight and his sun-streaked hair was dark with moisture.

He'd been swimming, Autumn thought, suddenly recalling the many times she had dived cleanly into the water to race him to the float. He'd always won and she'd always been furious. How many times had she lain on that old wooden float, breathless from

10

exertion and so angry that she could have heated the entire cove with a touch of her hand? And then within moments she had been laughing, swearing that she would beat him one day. She never had, though, and she'd long since forgotten why she'd been so determined to win. Funny, how a once all-important ambition could become unimportant.

Autumn stepped onto the dock and walked closer to where Cade was working. Her sandals flipped silently against her heels, protesting the rough surface beneath them. As she came up beside the sailboat she let her gaze stray from Cade to the sleek lines of the boat.

Shiny new and expensive, she decided. Built for racing, but seaworthy for a trip to the Caribbean, providing the crew numbered two or less. It was a beauty, but Autumn felt a twinge of sadness that this new boat had replaced *The Seasons,* the boat on which Cade had taught her to sail.

Slowly her eyes moved back to him and her lips curved a greeting. "Need some help?"

She watched the tension that rippled across his shoulders, noted the stillness that settled over his movements, and then heard his half-whispered question. "Autumn?"

He sounded so disbelieving that she gave a husky laugh and immediately he twisted on his heels to see her. "Autumn," he repeated, his voice stronger, but oddly cautious, as if he weren't sure it was really she.

He straightened slowly and her eyes were drawn to the dark hair that curled in damp profusion across his chest. She couldn't stop her gaze from

11

dropping to the snug fit of his wet cutoffs and the long sinewy legs that extended below the hems. Had she noticed and forgotten what a wonderful physique he possessed? No, she wouldn't have forgotten, so she must have been youthfully blind before.

Her eyes returned to his face, to the well-remembered angles and intricate pattern of character lines that defined the experience of his thirty-six years. There were barely discernible threads of silver at his temples, but surely that was only a trick of the sunlight. Still, he seemed different, somehow older than she remembered, endearingly familiar and yet almost a stranger. Silly thought. She'd known Cade forever. How could he be a stranger?

Then despite the several feet that separated her from him, Autumn recognized the blue mischief of his eyes. A small sigh of relief eased from her throat. Cade hadn't changed.

Realizing that he was assessing the changes in her, too, she resisted the impulse to pat the fashionable feather-cut of her hair. Cade wouldn't like it. Or maybe he would. At least he couldn't complain about the color, she thought as her memory replayed his horror on the day years ago when she'd dyed the vibrant October shades to an unbecoming black. She smiled now at her own adolescent foolishness and clasped her hands loosely. The silence was a comfortable exchange between friends and she simply waited for him to speak.

"Hello, Autumn. You're a long way from home, aren't you?"

Warmed by the sound of his voice, she shook her

head and made a slow pirouette. "Home is the sailor, home from the sea and, as you can see, I'm home, safe and sound, from the big city."

His smile was a long time in coming. It lacked the roguish slant she remembered, but more than made up the difference in sheer masculine appeal. "It looks as if you just brought the city with you."

Autumn tilted her chin in defense of her designer clothes and the easy elegance with which she wore them. "Is that any way to welcome the best first mate who ever crewed for you? In case you've forgotten, Kincade O'Connor, you would never have won the Cambridge Regatta if it hadn't been for me."

"Same old Autumn," he said from his slightly elevated position on the boat deck. "Stubbornly determined that you won that race single-handed, even though it was my experience, my skill and—"

"And your boat." Autumn finished the sentence for him and laughed at the memories it evoked. Companionable amusement chipped away at the years that separated them, and she felt suddenly more at ease. Her gaze dropped to the polished sheen of the deck below his feet. "I'll bet you could win the Cup single-handedly with this. She looks fast."

"She is." He surveyed the boat with an air of pride. "Want to come for a sail?"

"I'd love it." Eagerness faded, though, as Autumn followed his downward gaze. The tips of her Italian sandals peeped from beneath loose-fitting, wine-colored trousers that matched the braided scarf belted at her waist. Her deep burgundy tunic delineated her softly curving femininity with casual understatement. She could have walked into the most exclusive restaurant on the Eastern shore without a second thought, but sailing . . . With a wry lift of her brow Autumn met his laughing eyes. "How about tomorrow?"

"I have to work tomorrow, Autumn. Have you been gone so long you've forgotten what Mondays are like at the store?" He wiped his hands on the rag he held, tossed it to the deck, then jumped lightly down beside her. His deck shoes made a whispery sigh when they struck the wood, and Autumn felt an odd, breathy pressure in her lungs. At close range Cade was bigger, taller, and more male than she remembered and a ridiculous wish that she was meeting him for the first time whisked through her mind.

"Mondays." Silently scolding that unexpected flight of fancy, she nodded in a knowing way. "Inventory lists, weekend backorder forms, restocking the shelves, phone orders from the marinas, at least one minor catastrophe in the shipping department. Mondays at Eastport Boat Supply isn't something easily forgotten, Cade. No matter how long I've been gone."

"And how long has it been since you ran away from home?" His tone was light, teasing, and somehow irritating.

"Five years, seven months, give or take a few weeks. And I didn't run away."

"That's right, I remember. You left to 'follow your dreams.'" He brushed a palm against the waist of his shorts and slipped his thumb inside a pocket.

"Dancing until dawn, sleeping until afternoon, tasting the opulent life of the idle rich—all the things you used to daydream about."

Autumn clasped her hands a little tighter and thought that once she would have pushed him off the pier for using such a superior, I'm-older-and-wiser tone of voice. Well, she was older and wiser now, but if he continued this perplexing attitude, she just might have to reconsider.

"I never dreamed that people really lived such a day-to-day fantasy, Cade. During the two years I was Mrs. Colburn's personal secretary, I got to travel extensively. I spent a Christmas on the Riviera. I've been to the Louvre, the New York City Ballet, opening nights on Broadway. It was exciting and fascinating and I'll never regret taking the opportunity that was offered to me."

He looked past her shoulder for a few seconds before his eyes returned, reluctantly it seemed, to hers. "Sounds like the sort of lifestyle you always wanted. I'm surprised you can find time for a visit."

"I'm not visiting now, Cade. I'm home to stay." She was prepared to smile, maybe even laugh, at his expected surprise, but she had never anticipated the solemn tightening of his jaw. Her pleasure in this homecoming crumbled a little and she looked searchingly into his eyes, past the forget-me-not blue to the man she'd always known as her best friend. He had changed. Or perhaps the change lay within her. Autumn knew only that the comfortable, easy camaraderie between them was gone and she felt oddly lost without it.

"So, Autumn Tremayne, world traveler, ingenue

15

in disguise, comes home to stay. That ought to make the Eastport headlines." He was teasing in much the same way he'd always teased her, but it wasn't really the same at all.

"I really doubt that," she said with a deliberately pointed look. "It's hard to believe the newspaper would be interested when my best friend is noticeably unimpressed."

His eyes met hers in a silent struggle that she couldn't quite understand, and then his expression softened, the smile on his lips finally settling in his eyes. "I'm impressed, Autumn. And surprised. And sorry that I didn't greet you properly to begin with." His big hands cupped her shoulders and drew her to him.

She went into his arms without resistance, knowing he was going to kiss her hello as he'd done countless times in the past. But as her palms came to rest on his chest, a fugitive shiver of longing slid unexpectedly down her back. The undiluted sensuality of him caught her completely off-guard and her belated protest came too late. "Cade . . . ?"

His lips came to hers in that fragile moment of parted awareness . . . a gentle, light, affectionate touch that stated their relationship in a brief fragment of time. More than friends, less than lovers. It was the way he'd always kissed her, yet now her lips trembled beneath his with the sure and sudden knowledge that it was no longer the way she wanted him to kiss her.

Confused by her reaction, Autumn pulled back. He released her at once, his hands sliding the length of her arms in casual, but lingering relinquishment.

Her eyes sought his hesitantly, searching for an elusive answer that was nowhere to be found in the smiling gaze he returned to her. "Welcome home, Sprite," he said evenly.

With his use of her nickname the panicky flutter in her stomach subsided. A measure of perspective returned and she decided she was imagining a tempest in a teapot. "You haven't called me that in years, Cade. I thought I'd outgrown it long ago."

"You never outgrow nicknames. Especially when I can remember the first time you trotted down the path, all arms and legs and eyes under a mop of coppery hair. I never thought anything so small could contain so many questions." His voice warmed with reminiscence. "Then you challenged me to a race, dove off the end of the dock, and swam to the float as if you were a water sprite. How old were you then? Four, five years old?"

"Six," she answered, uncomfortably conscious of how very young she must seem to him even now. Shifting away from the thought, she took a few steps forward and placed a loving hand against the boat house. "And twenty-one years later this is still my favorite spot in all the world. It feels good to be back." She felt his disquieting regard and knew he was in some way displeased.

"Ross didn't tell me you were coming."

It sounded a little like an accusation and Autumn looked over her shoulder at Cade. "He didn't know. I just decided a week ago and . . . well, here I am."

Cade agreed with a nod. "Yes, here you are. So what are you planning to do now?"

Eager confidences sprang to mind, but Autumn found herself hesitant to mention any of her fledgling ambitions. "I'm not really sure," she said in compromise. "Maybe an investment in a local business, something where my experience will be—"

"Experience?" His short laugh was edged with skeptical amusement. "Eastport isn't exactly a haven for rich socialites looking for paid companions, you know."

She swung to face him, annoyed that he had placed her on the defensive. "I was never a 'paid companion,' Cade. I worked for Mrs. Colburn as her personal secretary, a demanding job with many responsibilities. And then three years ago I took over the position of merchandising manager for the Colburn chain of boutiques. Both jobs gave me valuable experience in dealing with the public and in managing a business. How could you believe I would waste six years of my life? You, Cade, of all people, should know me better than that."

"You've been gone a long time, Autumn, with hardly more than a half dozen weekend visits in between. It's been at least three years since I last saw you. The few letters you sent were little more than postcards describing someplace you'd been. How can you expect me to know everything about you?"

"I don't!" she snapped, but she knew that she had expected him to. The fact that she hadn't had a real conversation with him since she'd left, the fact that he had seldom answered the brief, overly cheerful letters she'd sometimes written, shouldn't have made such a difference. It was shared experiences and the affinity of spirit that marked the boundaries of their relationship, not the amount of time spent together.

Wasn't that the best thing about a friend you'd known all your life? No matter how long you'd been apart, there was never any need for pretense or explanation. There was just the understanding and acceptance that come with years of knowing each other. With a sigh Autumn calmed her irritation and wished fleetingly for the uncomplicated past when awkwardness had never intruded between them.

"I missed you." He was beside her, looking out across the quietly rippling water. With his hands lounging in his hip pockets, he made no move to touch her, but she knew he was reaching for a common bond, a familiar harmony of thoughts. "It's been . . . quiet since you left, Autumn."

She put her hands behind her and leaned against the coarse siding. Lonely. She had thought he was going to say it had been lonely without her and she suddenly knew the name of the haunting, restless feeling that had followed her all over the globe. Loneliness. For a long time it had lain dormant, obscured by the glittering call of each new horizon, but she had always known it was there, that silent, unobtrusive feeling that she didn't really belong. Once she had belonged here, but Autumn wondered if that was still true. She was home again, yet there was an emptiness inside her that she couldn't explain.

"At this rate, it will continue to be quiet around

here." Cade's voice brought her attention full circle and she smiled softly, hesitantly.

His lips curved into a matching smile and her tension began to ease. "Give me time, Cade. I've been home only a couple of hours. It takes a while to organize noise. Remember how long it took me to plan my high school graduation party?" She patted the rough wall behind her. "The boat house shook with noise that day."

"The whole town shook that day."

"As I recall, you did your part, Cade. Every girl at the party was madly in love with you."

"Except one."

Her eyes widened with sudden question, but he looked away, still smiling, still puzzlingly different. "I was the only one who knew you were just teasing." She paused and tilted her head inquiringly. "Is that why you seem so . . . so unapproachable today? Has it been too long since you had someone to tease, Cade?"

He pinned her with cool regard. "I haven't exactly been friendless all these years, Autumn. There are people who find me very 'approachable,' and when I want someone to tease, I invite . . . friends . . . out for a sail."

Why the hesitation? Autumn wondered, and then asked lightly, "Anyone I know?"

"No," he answered, piquing her interest by his very brusqueness.

"How can you be so sure, Cade?" She couldn't resist teasing him a little. "Eastport isn't that big and I know most of—"

"Jay and his mother moved here from the Midwest. You don't know them, Autumn."

Her desire to tease him vanished. "I'll have to meet Jay . . . and his mother . . . now that I'm home. Especially if they're frequent visitors to our dock." His only response was a noncommittal lift of his brow and, against her better judgment, Autumn pressed the issue. "Of course, if they are frequent visitors, it would be nice to know a little about them first."

His sigh was half-impatience, half-resignation. "Jay Meyers is a sturdy five-year-old who makes me wish that I had a son."

The warmth in his voice pricked her heart like a splinter pricks the skin. She hated the tight knot of curiosity in her stomach, but she had to ask, "And his mother?"

"Marilynda." Cade looked past Autumn, his mouth forming a smile that she knew wasn't meant for her.

"Marilynda?" Autumn repeated the name thoughtfully, disliking the way the lyrical syllables rolled easily on her tongue, disliking even more the way Cade had made them sing.

"She's been the office manager at the store for about two years now. She's efficient, organized—"

"Married?" Autumn hated her own lack of tact, but she couldn't stop the question.

"No," he answered evenly, "she's a widow."

"Oh." A dozen different reactions swirled through her mind, puzzling, unsettling reactions that culminated in another tactless question. "Is she the special woman in your life, Cade?" Autumn waited for his answer, her heartbeat a dull vibration in her chest, her gaze never leaving his unrevealing profile. She waited, afraid she would see that secret smile again.

An osprey called loudly as it skimmed across the cove, piercing the stillness with its brusque cry. Unwillingly Autumn turned to watch its flight, wishing that Cade had answered her, knowing that by his silence, he had. The osprey winged from sight and Autumn thought that auld lang syne sailed with it.

With determination and a ready smile she looked at Cade. "I suppose I should get back to the house. Lorna and the kids were gone when I arrived, but they should be back by now. It's been so long since I saw my niece and nephew and my sister-in-law, too, for that matter, I'm really anxious to"—she lost the train of her vacant thoughts and paused—"to see them."

Cade shifted to face her, his expression a study of friendly interest. "Lorna has always said she and Ross hoped you'd come back and live with them some day, but I don't believe either of them thought it would ever happen. I'm not sure I believe it now."

Autumn wasn't sure she believed it either. This half-sad welcome certainly was not the homecoming she'd imagined. "Would it seem more real if I challenged you to a race?"

"I'm afraid to accept," he said with a grin. "You may have been training all these years just so you can beat me to the float by a dozen strokes or more."

"You'd win, Cade, just like always." With a wry

shrug she moved away from the boat house. "Don't you know that heroes never lose?" She began walking toward the main path, expecting him to fall into step beside her. When he didn't, she stopped and glanced over her shoulder. He looked as if he had no intention of walking anywhere with her.

She pushed a reluctant laugh from her throat. "That was a setup, Cade. Didn't you recognize my subtle effort to lull you into a sense of security? The next time I race you to the float, I fully intend to win."

After what seemed a very long moment he winked at her. A wink that made her feel better and worse—better, because of its reassuring memories, worse, because it made her feel childishly young. She watched him lift a hand in good-bye before he moved to the boat and stepped aboard.

Following the path from the dock to the boxhedge that marked the official boundary of O'Connor-Tremayne property, Autumn slipped through an opening in the shrub. She had always considered the hedge a prickly nuisance that begrudged her entrance to the other side of the fence, but today it seemed appropriate. Something had definitely pricked her high spirits and, with a frown, she admitted that Cade, and only Cade, was responsible.

Ross had been glad to see her, eager to make her at home in the house that legally belonged to them both. Lorna would be pleased too. Autumn didn't doubt the sincerity of their welcome or her place in their family circle. It was Cade's lack of enthusiasm for her return, his whole puzzling attitude, that bothered her, left her feeling like an outsider.

The leather strap of her sandal tugged irritably at her heel and she reached down to strip the shoes from her feet. She would snag her nylons, of course, but it didn't seem important. Dangling the sandals from her fingertips, Autumn remembered running barefoot across the lawn and wished that she hadn't outgrown that carefree innocence. If she were still the child of yesterday, she would have been able to coax Cade into a real welcome, no matter what sort of mood he was in.

From almost the first moment of meeting him she had tagged his footsteps like a faithful puppy, incessantly chattering to him. Heaven alone knew why he'd put up with her then, or later, when she'd been so adolescently awkward. Perhaps he had thought of her as a pesky little sister, although she'd never considered him as an older brother. He had bullied her at times, encouraged her at others. He had teased her, flattered her, and often ignored her, but she'd always known she could depend on him. The friendship between them was something she'd never thought to question. She had simply accepted it as her right. Cade loved her and, with childish faith, she'd believed he always would.

White clouds scooted aimlessly in the late August sky. Autumn watched them, her thoughts drifting in the same disorderly pattern. *You might as well face it*, she told herself finally. *Things aren't the same anymore. Cade is different. You're different. Nothing stays the same, you know that.*

Of course she knew, but in her secret heart Autumn hadn't thought it possible that his feelings for her could change. Always his friendship had been there to support her. He had been her confidant, her trusted advisor, the only one she had ever been able to really talk to—until now.

She had been starry-eyed when she'd left, determined to discover the end of the rainbow. She'd been too naively young to know that what she longed for was something she already possessed. It had taken a long time for her to realize that home was the best place to be. Had she selfishly expected everything and everyone she loved to remain the same? Frozen in time until she chose to return and appreciate what she'd once scorned?

She breathed deeply of the fragrant air. The sweet scent of home surrounded her, the smell of salt water and trees and fresh air. It was Cade's scent, reminiscent of his smile. In her mind's eye she saw him as he'd looked today, standing on the new sailboat, his body lean, muscular, and glistening wet in the sunlight.

Today, for the first time, she'd seen him as more than a friend. And today she'd heard him speak another woman's name in a quiet, special way. A totally useless teardrop fell down her cheek and punctuated her melancholy sigh. "Welcome home, Autumn," she said aloud to no one in particular.

Cade sat back on his heels and frowned heavily at the sailboat's forward deck. It gleamed with the furious and largely unnecessary polishing he'd just given it. He had rubbed it as if, by some miracle, he could also rub the image of Autumn Tremayne from his thoughts.

He had told himself dozens of times that she would never come back to stay. He'd promised himself a thousand times that even if she did, it wouldn't matter. But when he'd seen her, heard the husky voice he remembered so well, he had known it still mattered.

God! It still mattered.

Cade pushed the rag over the deck once again and stared blindly at his hand, but he kept seeing her coppery-bronze hair, glinting gold in the sun, and her brown eyes that danced with her enthusiasm for life. Autumn.

He'd missed her. Until today he hadn't let himself acknowledge it. When she'd left home he decided he'd wasted enough time waiting for her to grow up and into love with him. If it had been meant to happen, she would have stopped thinking of him as an older brother long ago. She wouldn't have needed to leave home; she would have realized that she belonged with him.

Cade had never completely understood his feelings for Autumn. At first, she'd been simply a precocious child who, for some inexplicable reason, could coerce him into laughter when he least intended to laugh. With all the fierce devotion at her command she had loved him, looked up to him, believed he could do anything from bandaging a scraped knee to sailing to the farthest star.

He didn't know when he'd first realized that her role in his life was changing. But somewhere along the way to becoming a beautiful, bewitching woman, Autumn had captured his heart and he'd waited patiently, foolishly, for her to give her heart to him in return.

He had never told her. At first she'd been too young, then as the age difference diminished in importance, he'd thought she wasn't ready to accept more than his friendship. So he'd waited. He'd been the companion she wanted, the hero of all her daydreams, and he'd asked nothing in return. Like a fool he'd loved her and he'd thought she would know it when the time was right. But that time had never come.

And now. Now that he'd finally convinced himself that there was no point, no future in loving her, she was back. He wondered what had precipitated the move. Autumn had always been impulsive, but he couldn't quite believe this homecoming was a spur-of-the-moment decision. Something must have happened and the most likely "something" was a man.

Cade hated that idea, hated the very thought of Autumn in another man's arms, but he couldn't discount it as sheer speculation. She was more lovely than he'd ever imagined she would be, and she had the look of a woman who'd known love and lost it. And when he'd kissed her, with considerable self-restraint, he had recognized her trembling response, that tentative seeking of reassurance.

Flinging aside the rag, he stood and balanced himself against the sway of the sailboat. *Damn you, Autumn,* he thought. *I can't nurse you through a broken heart. I don't want to be your hero anymore. I don't even want you here.*

His lips formed a tight line as he battled the impulse to shout his thoughts to the wind. Maybe if she heard, she would leave him to the peaceful, contented pattern of his life. Maybe he would forget her. Maybe in time he could love Marilynda.

Is she the special woman in your life? The memory of Autumn's question was a soft hurt inside him. He'd let her believe it was true, let her walk away thinking that someone else had become more important to him than she. Why had he done that?

Hell, he wanted it to be true. He wanted a family; he needed a woman who could give him something in return, a woman who saw him as a man and not as the heroic answer to her every need.

He couldn't blame Autumn for her attitude toward him. He'd spoiled her, taught her to depend on him, but he'd always expected that one day she would grow up. Maybe if he could go back, he would do things differently. He had loved her, he thought with a derisive frown, not wisely, but too well. If only she'd stayed away another year, maybe he could have welcomed her home with no lingering traces of regret.

But no matter. Autumn was back, but he wouldn't let it make any difference.

"Welcome home, Sprite," he said aloud before he forced his whole attention back to the boat.

CHAPTER TWO

Plump cherries bubbled a deep, delectable red beneath the criss-cross pie crust. Autumn eased the oven door shut, wiped her palms on the seat of her jeans, and glanced at the kitchen sink. Dishes, rolling pin, pans, and measuring cups cluttered the view, but for some incomprehensible reason, she felt like humming.

Once she would have cringed at the sight and begun immediately to convince her mother that it was really Ross's turn to clean up. Not that that tactic had always proved successful, but it had worked often enough to warrant a try.

Autumn pushed the sleeves of her blouse higher up her arms and advanced on the sink. Even if Ross were home today, she wouldn't have allowed him anywhere near those dishes. It had been a long time since she'd had either the time or the inclination to run a sink full of hot, soapy water and wash dishes by hand.

She had been spoiled by the Colburns' brand of luxury, she freely admitted that. But from the moment she met Lucinda Colburn and her son, Richard, Autumn had been swept into their lives and lifestyle like a leaf caught in a strong breeze. It had been another world for her. A world in which someone else was paid to do the dishes and the cooking and the cleaning and every other household chore. Of course, she, too, had been paid by the Colburns, but her position had placed her on a higher echelon and kept her thoughts from going anywhere near the kitchen.

Absently turning on the faucet, she remembered how easily she had adjusted. Too easily, perhaps. Already those years seemed unreal to her. This, the home of her childhood, was real. Autumn pursed her lips in a wry smile. The dishes were certainly real and adjustment to the "real" world was as simple as running water into the sink. At the moment, though, she couldn't think of another thing she'd rather do. It had been too long since she'd felt so domestic, so contented, and so "at home."

Ross and Lorna had felt guilty about going away for the weekend and nothing Autumn had said could persuade them that she honestly didn't mind. She'd even insisted that they leave Beth and Brian at home with her, stating with perfect truth that she hardly knew her niece and nephew and this was a golden opportunity to remedy that.

As she turned off the water and reached for a dishrag, Autumn hoped that her brother and sister-

30

in-law were enjoying their trip to Baltimore as much as she was enjoying being in charge of the house. She had found pleasure in the most simple tasks—making beds, cooking, washing dishes. Not that she thought the pleasure wouldn't fade with repetition; she was certain it would. But for the moment it was satisfying to know that she hadn't forgotten the basic how-to of homemaking.

Beth's blond ponytail bobbed happily as she skipped through the doorway. Her nose wrinkled in an exaggerated effort to inhale the aroma of cherry pie. "Is it ready yet?"

"Not until the buzzer sounds," Autumn answered. "Would you like to help wash dishes?"

Beth came closer to eye the sudsy sink. "You're supposed to rinse the dishes and put them in the dishwasher," she informed with six-year-old wisdom. "Didn't you know that, Aunt Autumn?"

"I guess I forgot, but this is more fun anyway." Autumn pulled a chair from the table and scooted it to the counter. "Here, now you can help."

Without a moment's hesitation Beth scrambled onto the chair and stuck her fingers into the mound of suds. She looked so blissfully disbelieving that Autumn couldn't resist a smile. "Where's your brother?" she asked.

Blue eyes took on a glimmer of self-protection. "He's watching cartoons. Don't call him in here, Aunt Autumn. He'll just make a mess."

With a nod of understanding, Autumn determinedly kept her gaze from the suds that were even now dripping down the front of the cabinet. After all she, too, knew what it meant to be an older

31

sister, and Brian was probably happier watching cartoons anyway.

When the telephone rang Beth jumped from the chair like a coiled spring, splattering soapy water across the floor as she ran to answer it. The phone jangled again and the oven timer buzzed loudly just as Cade, followed by an incessantly talkative Brian, walked into the kitchen.

Autumn glanced from the oven to the phone to her niece to her nephew to Cade, lingered just long enough to see him lift his shoulder in a don't-look-at-me-I-just-got-here shrug, before she stepped forward and clicked off the timer. Grabbing a potholder, she opened the oven door and slid the pie out. With a tiny smile of triumph she placed it on the counter and turned, thinking that at the very least, she would receive a round of applause.

There wasn't even a single handclap. Only the high-pitched voices of Beth, talking into the phone, and of Brian, talking to anyone who might be listening. Cade's blue eyes made a casual sweep of the confusion before settling on Autumn with ill-concealed amusement. "Busy day at the Betty Crocker kitchen?" he asked.

She returned his amusement with a pointedly sweet smile. "No one likes a smartas—aleck," she said. "And don't try to deny that you came over only because you thought I'd be wandering aimlessly from room to room, not knowing where to begin."

"This looks like a good place to start," he observed dryly.

"Be my guest." Autumn tossed a dishrag in his

direction and watched him catch it with one hand. Had he always been so agile? Her gaze wandered along the muscled curve of his arm to the white knit pullover to the crisp fit of new jeans to the leather ties of his Topsider shoes and back to the laughter in his eyes. The breath in her lungs became painfully tight and she released it softly. Had he always been so attractive?

"You have a warped sense of hospitality, Miss Tremayne." He tossed the rag into the sink before he slipped the watch from his wrist and handed it to Autumn. "Whatever happened to 'Hello, Cade. How nice to see you. Can I get you something to drink?'"

Autumn smiled as she accepted his watch and laid it safely on the table. "Hello, Cade. How nice to—"

"Aunt Autumn," Beth interrupted with magnified impatience. "It's for you."

Reluctantly Autumn turned from Cade to the telephone receiver that dangled in Beth's hand. As she reached for it, Beth whispered clearly, "It's a *man.*"

Feeling suddenly and unaccountably guilty, Autumn put the receiver to her ear and turned her back to Cade, as if she had something to feel guilty about. "Hello," she murmured hoarsely, then she made herself turn again and face the reason for her discomfort. Cade seemed oblivious, though, his total attention on Beth, Brian, and the dishes.

"Hello," Autumn repeated, more loudly than she'd intended.

"Ah! Sweet mystery of life, at last I've found you."

33

With a helpless sigh Autumn smiled. "God, Richard, don't sing." Cade looked up at that, she noticed, and she silently willed him not to listen.

"I can't sing," Richard said cheerfully. "Without you my heart is broken into a thousand fragments." He paused to give a dramatic sigh. "But the parade marches on, you know. How are things back at the marina?"

"I don't know." She dropped her gaze to the floor. That was one of the things she did feel guilty about. "I haven't been to the marina."

"Been spending your days outfitting the local yachtsmen at the store, have you?"

Damn! She could feel Cade listening as if he could hear everything Richard was saying, as if he, too, was wondering why she hadn't made even a brief appearance at the store. "No, I haven't been to the store—yet." She tacked on the last word purposefully and watched Cade's brow rise.

Richard murmured a hum of speculation. "All right, I give. Where have you been?"

"The kitchen." Her answer was automatic as she watched Cade bend and lift Brian to stand beside Beth on the chair. Against the children's fairness, his dark hair made an appealing contrast.

"God, Autumn," Richard said with a laugh, "that sounds too exciting to be true."

It wasn't exciting, she thought, just nice. And she suddenly felt sorry for Richard, who had probably never washed a dish in a sink full of soap bubbles. "I baked a pie," she told him. "Cherry. Your favorite." Cade's blue eyes regarded her solemnly for a min-

34

ute. Cherry pie was his favorite. She had no idea if Richard even liked pie.

"Sounds better and better." Richard's voice softened. "I miss you, Autumn. When are you coming home?"

Home. Her gaze traced the line of Cade's smile as he teased Beth with a tug of her ponytail. Brian blew suds onto Cade's shirt sleeve to gain attention. Cade laughed, the children giggled, and Autumn felt left out, an outsider looking in.

"Autumn?" Richard persisted.

"I am home." Her tone lacked conviction and she turned her back to the room before she spoke again. "How's the new merchandising manager working out?"

"She's doing your job like she was born to it, but she can't bake a pie worth a plug nickel. All things considered, I'd say she has great-looking legs."

Autumn laughed and Cade felt the tension stretching inside him. What had "Richard" said to make her laugh like that? And when had that hint of throaty seduction crept into her laughter? Damn, he was jealous of a voice at the other end of the phone; he was envious of the recipient of Autumn's amusement. How stupidly adolescent! He had no right to be jealous, no right to feel like an outsider because she was talking to someone else.

Not someone else. Richard, who liked cherry pie. Cade suddenly hated cherry pie and he wondered what he was doing in the Tremaynes' kitchen . . . besides the dishes. How had he let her talk him into that? He rinsed a glass and set it on the counter to dry, knowing that he had volunteered without a

35

solitary protest. He had walked through the doorway and fallen into a trap of his own making.

For a captivating instant, when he'd first seen her against the backdrop of the messy kitchen, her hair tousled, shirt sleeves rolled unevenly to her elbows, floury handprints on her jeans, and her feet bare, he had imagined that this was his home, his kitchen . . . his Autumn.

"They're gone." Cade snapped his attention to the mournful face of Brian, who was staring indignantly at the dishwater. "The bubbles are gone."

Beth leaned closer to watch the last of the suds dissolve. "Let's make more," she said to Cade, and he couldn't help but touch her nose with a teasing finger. Beth looked more like her mother than her aunt, but something in her trusting expression reminded him of Autumn.

"I have a better idea." He rinsed the last spoon and released the stopper to let the water drain. "Let's go on a picnic."

The suggestion met with instantaneous and boisterous approval. Brian, followed closely by his sister, bounced to the floor and raced to his aunt. "We're going on a picnic." "Hang up the phone, Aunt Autumn. Cade said we're going on a picnic." "Can we take the soccer ball? I'll go and get it." "No, let me get it!"

It was impossible to distinguish who said what amidst the excited chatter and Autumn placed her hand over the receiver to ask for a moment of quiet, but before she could get a word out, Beth raced out the doorway with Brian at her heels.

Autumn looked to Cade in confusion and found

herself unexpectedly entangled in the twilight uncertainty of his eyes. Tension crackled through her like static electricity and was instantly gone, leaving only a trace of awareness in its wake. Richard continued talking, but she heard only the shallow sounds of her own breathing.

Cade broke the contact and began rinsing out the sink, as if he had noticed nothing unusual in that split-second exchange. And why not? There had been nothing unusual about it. She must have imagined the odd look in his eyes. Bending her head in concentration, she tried to draw Richard's words into a coherent pattern in her mind. God, it was unbearably warm in the kitchen. She must have forgotten to turn off the oven.

Richard paused expectantly and, from somewhere, Autumn pulled out a laugh that could pass for a response. Apparently satisfied, he laughed too. "It's wonderful to hear your voice again," he said. "I'm looking forward to seeing you. Eastport sounds like such an 'alive' place, I can hardly wait to get there. And I'll expect you to bake a pie for me. What kind did you say is my favorite?"

"Cherry."

"Right. Cherry. I'll have to remember that."

Autumn frowned and zeroed in on a more important point. "When are you going to get here?"

Something clattered loudly to the floor behind her and she turned her frown on Cade. He shrugged an apology as he bent to retrieve the metal lid.

"I don't know, Autumn," Richard replied. "Probably in a couple of weeks or three or four. I'll surprise you."

"Wonderful, I'll love it." Her smile of relief was genuine, although she wasn't sure why she'd even worried. It would be nice to see Richard and it would be a surprise. In the more than five years she'd known him, he had constantly surprised her in one way or another.

"That's easy for you to say. It takes a great deal of plotting to arrive unexpectedly, you know."

"Oh, Richard," Autumn said on a breath of laughter. "What would I do without you to keep life exciting?"

"You'd bake cherry pies. Good-bye, Autumn. I'll love you forever."

"Or at least until the next time you see the new merchandising director with the great legs."

"Oh, at least until then," he conceded. "But what can I say?"

"Good-bye, Richard." She turned toward the steady regard of blue eyes on her denim-clad legs. At Richard's final good-bye she replaced the phone and met Cade's lazy smile with a disapproving tilt of her chin.

He slipped his hands into the back pockets of his jeans, oblivious to her silent criticism. "There's nothing wrong with your legs, Autumn."

"I know, Cade. There's obviously nothing wrong with your hearing either."

His smile remained unchanged and he was definitely not stricken with guilt. "You couldn't really expect me not to eavesdrop when you made it so easy."

"With all the noise you and the kids made, it's a wonder I could hear anything."

"They were excited. We're going on a picnic."

"We are?"

Cade raised his brows. "Don't you want to go?"

Autumn pulled a hand across her forehead and walked to the oven to be sure it had been turned off. "Do I have to provide the food?"

"Only dessert," he said, subtly eyeing the pie as he moved to lean against the counter. "Unless, of course, you're saving it for your boyfriend."

Her gaze narrowed in slow annoyance on the teasing edge of his smile. "I outgrew 'boys' years ago, Cade, and by the time Richard finally arrives at my door, that particular pie will be ancient history. Now, if you can refrain from making any more annoying remarks about 'boyfriends,' I will graciously accept your invitation"—she caught his sidelong glance at the pie—"on behalf of myself and the prospective dessert."

The curve of his lips deepened and warmed her irritation with friendly affection. "You never used to be so touchy, Autumn."

Which was perfectly true, she admitted, but things were different now. She wasn't sure why, but she knew that things were different.

"Let's go!" Brian raced into the room, a soccer ball in one hand, a tennis racquet in the other.

"That looks like a dangerous combination, fella." Cade bent to confront Brian. "Let's make a deal. You leave the racquet here and we'll take Jay with us."

"Jay?" Brian's eyes sparkled with interest. "Oh,

boy." He whirled and raced from the room as fast as he'd entered it.

Autumn fought back the apprehension that had knotted her stomach at the mention of Jay's name and tried, unsuccessfully, to hide her disappointment. "The picnic isn't just for us?"

Cade looked up at her, then slowly straightened. "No, do you mind?"

"Of course not," she said quickly, too quickly. "I only—well, with Jay and his mother—don't you think three adults is one too many?"

"There won't be three adults. Marilynda wanted to catch up on some filing at the office, so I'm taking care of Jay for the afternoon. Now, the way I look at it, that adds up to three children, one adult, and one undecided."

Relief eased over her like a cooling shower and try as she might, Autumn couldn't contain a low laugh. "All right, Cade, but I'm warning you. Next time you have to be the adult and I get to be undecided."

His answering grin made her wonder how she could have ever stayed away so long.

Jay Meyers had the darkest eyes and the thickest lashes Autumn had ever seen. He was slight, small for his age, and excruciatingly polite—to her. With Cade he became as boisterous and bouncy as four-year-old Brian and as sassy as Beth.

It took Autumn the better part of the afternoon to understand the sense of frustration that met her every effort to win Jay's confidence. No matter what she said or did, he kept a careful distance between them. Ordinarily that wouldn't have bothered her a great deal, but it was obvious that Jay adored Cade, an emotion she could readily identify with and that, even on a purely subliminal level, should have made Jay her ally.

But it didn't. Jay watched her with caution, if not suspicion, and Autumn felt frustrated and overly sensitive and . . . jealous.

Yes. As she folded the picnic cloth and added it to the take-home sack of leftovers, she recognized the emotion. She was jealous, but it had little to do with five-year-old Jay. It had a lot to do, however, with Jay's mother.

If Marilynda Meyers had missed the picnic, her name certainly had not and for that Autumn could blame no one but herself. Seeing the easy relationship between Cade and Jay had whetted Autumn's curiosity about the relationship between Cade and Marilynda. But no matter how carefully her questions were composed, Cade's answers were just as carefully unrevealing. Cade was straightforward about the Meyerses in general, both mother and son, but disgustingly vague whenever the conversation turned the slightest bit personal. By the end of lunch Autumn wished he would simply come right out and tell her that he was in love with the woman.

Autumn sank to her knees in the middle of the quilt that was spread over the ground. It wasn't fair to blame Cade for the restless feeling inside her. There was no reason for him to confide in her, no reason for her to feel left out because he didn't choose to satisfy her curiosity. But she couldn't think of a single reason not to blame the absent

Marilynda for taking the gloss off what should have been a relaxing late August afternoon.

Sitting back on her heels, Autumn watched the rough-and-tumble soccer game taking place between Cade and the kids. Her inner tension mellowed at the sight of his long muscular legs as he gently maneuvered the ball around three pairs of wildly kicking feet. At some point Cade had stripped off his pullover and his shoulders glistened with the sheen of exertion.

Her gaze outlined the latent strength of his arms and traced the masculine slenderness of his hips. His every movement was concise, intriguing, and somehow more sensual than she remembered. Over the years, she'd thought of Cade as being tall, cute, nice-looking, and any number of other adolescent phrases, but she'd never before considered him in such a purely physical way.

When had he acquired that subtle male charisma, that indefinable essence that whispered new discoveries to her senses? When had she become so breathily aware of the man who was her friend? She shifted uncomfortably on the quilt, her thoughts scattering in self-defense.

"Aunt Autumn! Did you see that?" Beth pointed proudly to the soccer ball that was rolling with considerable speed toward the ditch at the far side of the park. "I kicked it."

"Good shot," Autumn called, letting her gaze return to Cade, who was watching the ball with a rueful frown.

"All right, Beth," he said. "You kicked it, you go get it."

42

As if he'd fired the starting gun, the boys took off in a dead run, leaving Beth to shrill a protest and set out in pursuit. Cade rubbed the back of his neck before he walked over to where Autumn was sitting and dropped down beside her. "Too many afternoons like this could result in a substantial donation to Planned Parenthood."

She shot him a skeptical look and he conceded with a weary sigh. "Maybe I'm just getting too old to play with other people's children. I always thought that by this time in my life I'd have at least three of my own."

Cade's children. Autumn closed her eyes to see them. Sons, with his sun-browned hair and crooked smile, his mannerisms, and his engaging blue eyes. Perhaps one would have brown eyes, like her. She shook her head then, trying to shake out her crazy thoughts. God, what was she thinking?

"It isn't too late, you know," she said casually, and had to struggle with each word to keep her voice from betraying her. "I've never understood why you've stayed single so long."

A sudden stillness closed around her as Cade turned a slow, unreadable gaze to her face. Her heart pounded with the emotion she saw in his expression, emotion that she recognized but did not really comprehend.

"It wasn't something I had much choice about, Autumn. Marriage isn't one of the things you can just decide to do."

"Come on, Cade, don't try to convince me you haven't had opportunities. I can't believe there's never been anyone who meant that much to you."

Cade speared unsteady fingers through his hair and thought about telling her the truth. The problem was that there had always been someone who meant too much.

What would she say if he told her? But it was absurd even to imagine her reaction. She was a beautiful woman who would forever see him through the eyes of a child. He couldn't shatter that touch of innocence in her any more than he could blind himself to the desire that even now trembled within him.

He looked up to see the children still some distance away. Beth was carrying the soccer ball like a trophy, and Cade could tell that Brian and Jay didn't like it. The stubborn tilt of that little-girl chin made him think of Autumn, and he forced the reminiscence to take shape in his mind.

"You've developed a bad habit, Cade, of dropping out in the middle of a conversation. In case you've forgotten, we were talking about why you haven't had the opportunity to get married."

Her husky voice made the resemblance waver for a moment, but he got a firm hold on it before he turned to her again. "You're too young for that kind of discussion. Ask me about it when you're sixty-five."

His standard answer over the years, Autumn thought on a ripple of irritation. It had always been his way of teasing her, of keeping her from knowing too much about his personal life. Until today, she'd never realized how annoying it was to be constantly reminded that he was older, wiser, more experienced. Even hearing the laughter that edged his

44

voice, even knowing he had no idea that she resented being treated like a child, she was annoyed, yet the very fact of her annoyance confused her.

"Cade, watch this!" Jay grabbed the ball and kicked it before a startled Beth quite knew what had happened. The soccer ball soared toward its target, catching Autumn squarely on the shoulder. Her soft gasp was more surprise than anything else, although her skin stung from the impact.

"Are you okay?" Cade moved to kneel beside her, touching her with concerned tenderness. His fingers were warmly caring through the thin fabric of her blouse, his eyes were deeply, intensely blue as he massaged her shoulder.

She turned her head to watch his therapy, but her cheek brushed against his knuckles and her lower lip felt the smooth texture of his skin. Her eyes flew to his in startled question as her thoughts spun into a new dimension of confusion.

For a timeless moment the world around her stopped and she saw only Cade, his face so near her own that the very air she breathed was filled with his warmth. It was as if he had never touched her before, as if the facets of their relationship caught a streak of fire and diffused into a new and daring design. Poised on the edge of that moment, Autumn was aware of a soft, churning ache inside her, conscious of the fragile thread of tension in his stillness.

Then there was a new touch, the insistent grip of reality as Jay pushed Cade's hand aside to replace it with his own. "I'm sorry," he said, his small voice hushed in apology. "I didn't mean to hit you."

The moment was gone as if it had never been.

45

She turned to the concern of dark eyes regarding her through heavy lashes. "I'm sorry," Jay repeated.

"It's all right," she reassured him as she patted his hand. "I should have been more careful in choosing a place to sit. Next time I'll try not to get in the way of the ball."

His uncertain smile made her effort worthwhile and she felt Cade's movements as he levered to his feet. She dared not look at him, afraid of the embarrassment she could feel descending around her.

Cade bent to retrieve his top, but Brian tackled him with fervor. "Let's play again, Cade." Never one to be left out, Beth wrapped herself around Cade's leg and added her persuasions to her brother's. "Come on, let's play soccer." With only slight hesitation, Jay jumped into the fray.

"All right, all right." Cade surrendered to defeat with an exasperated laugh. "Get the ball and we'll play one more game, but that's it. This is absolutely the last game."

Autumn sent a silent thank-you to the children for salvaging an extremely awkward moment. As she watched the "last" game stretch into two, she called out encouragement and advice, but steadfastly refused to get involved. How could she roughhouse with Cade? That would be all it would take to make her feel like a complete child.

She was going to have to come to grips with her imagination; that was all there was to it. It wasn't like her to act as she had done today. Maybe it was just the adjustment of being home, of a more relaxed way of life. Autumn frowned. Or maybe it was the changes she had found in Cade.

Relationships changed with time. She would have to accept that, and she would have to accept Marilynda and Jay as having a place, an important place, in Cade's life. It was natural, Autumn supposed, to feel a little jealous. All right, she conceded to her conscience, more than a little, but, after all, she had grown up believing that Cade belonged to her. He'd always been her hero and she had a proprietary interest in his happiness.

His laughter cut through the air to punctuate her conclusions. He certainly sounded happy now. If Cade were in love with Marilynda, then Autumn could only hope that everything worked out for them. But in her heart, she knew without having ever met her that Marilynda wasn't good enough for him.

What was she going to do when Cade was married to someone else? When he had a family of his own to take on picnics? God! She was becoming depressed and morose.

Anyone would think she wanted to spend the rest of her life taking her niece and nephew on outings. Her gaze settled lovingly on Beth, then Brian, turned to Jay, and finally found its way to Cade. If she had to share him, and of course she did, then she would be gracious about it. With a sigh of resignation Autumn wondered how Marilynda felt about cherry pie.

CHAPTER THREE

Autumn paused outside the glass-paned, bow window of Eastport Boat Supply. Displayed on the wide sill against the shadowy interior of the store was a clutter of sailing gadgetry filling every bit of available space. Apparently Cade was still in charge of dressing the window, she decided with a shake of her head, a task he was both unsuited for and uninterested in.

"No one walks into a boat supply because of something they see in the window," he'd always said, dismissing her suggestions that he clean up the display. She had wasted tons of breath trying to point out that not everyone who passed the store was a seafaring enthusiast, that there might—just might—be someone who would be intrigued by a few pieces of scrimshaw tastefully displayed in the window.

She stood there, looking in, remembering all the

hours she had spent inside wishing she were outside looking in, just as she was now. For years she had had the idea that life was passing by this window while day after day, after school and on Saturdays, she worked within the same four walls. Autumn touched the wooden window casing in belated apology and decided that from this point on, her love-hate relationship with Eastport Boat Supply would undergo a positive change.

The store and the marina were words that had shaped the foundations of her childhood. From the moment her father had joined his World War II buddy, Kent O'Connor, in partnership, from the day the Tremaynes had moved next door to the O'Connors, Autumn's future had been formed.

How often had her father tucked her in at night with a bedtime story that centered on the latest sales figures for Eastport, Inc.? Autumn smiled, remembering how Ross had listened in rapt attention while she had yawned and begged for a "real" story. But despite her blasé attitude, she had learned, just as Ross had, that the store and the marina were her heritage and they demanded both her time and energy. While Ross had early on shown an aptitude for the maintenance work done at the marina, Autumn had tried hard not to show any aptitude at all. But she had been assigned to the store nonetheless.

She had soon discovered the silver lining in that particular cloud—Cade. What she would have begrudged doing for herself, she did freely for Cade.

A breeze drifted around the corner of the store to catch in her hair. She breathed in its salty tang and remembered how often she had stood on the dock behind the store, daydreaming about the far horizon. Cade had just as often found her there, but he'd never scolded or reminded her there was work to be done. He'd simply been with her, not sharing her dreams, but supporting her right to seek them out.

She owed a great deal to Kincade O'Connor, Autumn thought as she pulled open the front door and stepped inside. Her senses merged with the sights, sounds, and smells of the store. It felt good, definitely right, and she wondered at the convoluted priorities of her youth. How had she failed to understand the satisfaction, the pride of ownership? Why had it been so hard to see that she belonged to this store, to this place, as surely as it belonged to her?

Of course only a quarter interest in the business was actually hers. At his father's death, Cade had assumed control of the O'Connor half of the partnership. Several years later Autumn and Ross had shared the other half when their father chose to retire and move—bag, baggage, and their mother— to Florida. Cade had continued as manager of the store, Ross had overseen the marina, and Autumn had followed her heart to the horizon.

"Autumn, when did you get in?" It was John, the shipping clerk, tall, lanky, balding, and with a grin to match the handshake that practically wrung her hand from her wrist. "Haven't seen you in a month of Sundays. 'Bout time you dropped in for a visit on your way to fame and fortune."

What a gadfly reputation she'd acquired during her absence, she thought, discreetly flexing her fingers as she withdrew them from his grasp. "How are you, John? And how's your family?"

"Fine. Just fine."

At his reply she smiled and let her gaze take in the familiar surroundings. Racks, shelves, and assorted tables held a wealth of equipment, everything from sailboat hardware to several styles of deck shoes. It wasn't exactly neat, but any clutter was due to the variety and the multitude of odds and ends required for boating. Autumn knew to the last nut and bolt just how well organized the stock actually was.

At the back of the large room was a door that opened into a storage area and to the right was a door leading to the office. When John was called back to his department, Autumn exchanged hellos with a few of the salespeople before making her way to the office.

It looked much the same as it always had, except for the new carpet, the woven-woods that had replaced venetian blinds at the windows, several healthy-looking plants, and six swivel chairs that Autumn strongly suspected were a matched set. The desks of the office personnel certainly looked the same, although there were new people behind them. She waved a greeting to the two employees she did recognize.

"May I help you?"

The smiling receptionist was new, Autumn thought, bringing the helpful smile into focus. "No, thank you, I'm—" Her gaze went past the receptionist to the name plate on the second desk from the front. MARILYNDA MEYERS, OFFICE MANAGER,

51

it read. Autumn looked across the neat desktop to an empty chair. Disappointment and relief eased the tight curve of her mouth and she turned back to the young receptionist. "I'm Autumn Tremayne. Is Cade here?"

"No, he isn't back from lunch yet, but you can wait if you like. I'm sure he'll be back soon."

Lunch? Autumn frowned at her watch. Almost three o'clock. Some lunch. Suspicion took her direct stare to the second desk from the front. The office manager appeared to be out to lunch, also, but Autumn tilted her chin and tactfully resisted asking that too obvious question. "I'll just look around in the store then." With that, Autumn retreated, wishing she had arrived earlier, but knowing that she probably wouldn't have been invited to lunch even if she had.

Restless, she wandered through the aisles and stopped beside the wooden railing that separated the display window from the rest of the store. She appraised the entire effect and found it less than appealing. Maybe she had worked in tandem with professional window dressers for too many months to overlook the possibilities here, but whatever the reason, Autumn knew she could improve Eastport Boat Supply simply by rearranging the window.

Dropping her purse into the pullout drawer beneath the railing, she looked around for an empty box. Then she proceeded to fill it as she emptied the window space. About halfway through, she stepped back to view the result with a critical eye. If the Colburns had had such a lovely Cape Cod–type of window in their main store, Autumn had little doubt it would have increased sales. Why, right now, if she had a few swimsuits to display in this particular window . . .

Inspiration came like a breath of wind on a summer day. Why not? Eastport offered little in the way of quality fashions and nothing at all like the trend-setting styles Autumn had in mind. It would be simple, just one corner of the store and some display space in the window. She whirled to appraise each individual corner before choosing. With a few modifications, shelf space could be added along each wall to accommodate the displaced stock and that would leave enough room for the mini-boutique she envisaged.

Already she could see the possibilities grow. Customers would respond well to outfitting themselves as well as their boats in the same store. She just knew it. She would hold the inventory to basic sailing clothes, swimwear, shorts and shirts for summer, warmer but not bulky outerwear for other seasons. Of course sales would be slow in winter, but with a few accessories, maybe some nice pieces of scrimshaw, the boutique should be able to hold its own.

Autumn smiled with enthusiasm. *Eastport Boat Supply and Boutique.* Well, maybe that was stretching inspiration too far, but it would work regardless of what they chose to call it. Cade, of course, would have to okay the idea and Ross, too, she supposed. But they would agree, even if she had to twist their arms to the breaking point.

Happily Autumn returned to the window, stepping up and over the railing to the inside. It had been a long time since she'd felt so excited. The idea was a perfect answer to her search for a business investment. It might be somewhat risky at first, but she knew merchandising and she knew that her experience gave her an edge on success. The boat supply store would benefit, and best of all she would be close enough to consult Cade about . . .

Her thoughts filtered into the realization that she was under observation. She looked outside to see Cade, watching her through the glass, laughter hovering at the corner of his mouth. Late afternoon sunlight tossed his hair with gold and etched the angles of his face in shadow. Blue eyes beneath questioning brows asked what she was doing to his window. She wrinkled her nose in reply and motioned him to join her.

As he turned toward the front entrance, Autumn noticed the crisp lines of his suit with surprise. She'd never before seen him dressed so formally on a workday. He'd always worn casual clothes, just like every other employee. Running a boat supply wasn't like having an office in downtown Baltimore. It often involved everything from repairing broken rigging to restocking the shelves. Autumn shifted position. At times even the display window had to be cleaned, and that was definitely not a job for a three-piece suit.

Carefully putting one foot over the railing and steadying herself with a hand on the wall, she backed out of the window. A patch of warmth came to rest on either side of her waist and Cade lifted her down. "If I didn't know better," he said, "I could almost believe I saw you working."

She turned, letting his hands exchange places at her waist, letting her good spirits bestow a smile. "If I didn't know better, I could almost believe you're wearing a suit." Her fingers ran teasingly along the lapels, liking the feel of the nubbed fabric, liking the smooth rise and fall of his chest, liking the aura of controlled strength beneath her touch. "Did you have a nice lunch? A nice, *long* lunch?"

"I got started late." He pursed his lips in grudging admission. "Didn't even leave the office until—"

"Ten after twelve?"

"Fifteen after, Miss Know-It-All. Besides, it was a working lunch."

"Hmmm. Where did you go? Bernie's?" Bernie's boasted the one and only sit-down dining room in Eastport. It had always been Cade's favorite place for a quick, good meal, but somehow Autumn knew it was not where he'd had lunch today.

"There's a new restaurant not too far from town," he explained easily. "Whitecliffs. Speciality of the house—Maryland blue crab. You'd love it, Autumn. Maybe I'll take you there someday."

"Maybe I'll let you . . . someday." She arched one brow in flirty challenge. "But I think you're trying to change the subject. Let's go back to the new restaurant, new suit, and long lunch. Sounds like there could be a woman involved. Are you trying to make me jealous, Cade?"

"Are you trying to make me think I could?" he countered, his hands leaving her sides suddenly cool and lonely. Her flirtatious mood drooped a little with the lessening of his smile. "I know better,

Autumn. Just like I know that whatever you're doing to my window, I'm not going to like it."

"What a vote of confidence, but just as a matter of interest, one-fourth of this window belongs to me."

"Really? Which fourth? And be careful how you answer. This could be a trick question."

"Complete with glass cleaner or dustrag, depending on which section I choose. *That* trick I remember." She tilted her head back, eagerness dancing impishly in her eyes. "But now I have a trick question for you. What will entice new customers into the store, increase sales, improve the appearance of our clientele, and will take only one small corner of floorspace?"

His eyes deepened to a cautious blue. "A hot tub?"

Autumn smiled and slid her palm down his jacket sleeve until she could take his hand in hers. "Come with me."

He resisted the tug she gave and Autumn turned to question his hesitation. As she encountered his shadowy gaze, an odd, trembling sensation coursed through her. It was a curious unfolding of emotions that parted her lips with a slow intake of air and drew her brows to a softly inquiring frown. Under the pretext of loosening his tie, Cade regained his hand and Autumn regained her equilibrium.

"Come on. Let me show you my brilliant idea." Striving for a lighter tone, she walked toward the corner she had in mind and hoped he'd follow. She knew that the simple act of taking his hand, something she'd done countless times before with never a passing thought, had annoyed him. It was childish to let that bother her, just as it was childish to have noticed his discomfort at her entirely innocent touch. But childish or not, it hurt just the same.

She stopped at the end of a long row of shelves and waited for him to join her. When he did, she made a broad sweep with her arm. "Imagine this, Cade. A store within a store. A mini-boutique, right here." She turned to him in her budding enthusiasm, then turned back to visualize her words. "It will be small in size, but not in quality. We'll offer only clothes practical for wearing on a boat—swimwear, shorts, shirts, easy-care slacks, comfortable clothing, but still everything will be brand-names, the latest fashions. 'Chic clothes for the discriminating sailor,' that sort of thing.

"I know exactly the type of merchandise I want and I also just happen to know where and how to get it." Laughter rippled through her voice and she clasped her hands in pleasurable excitement. "Can't you just see it? Everything for both boat and owner. A one-stop shop, so to speak." Glancing at his pensive expression, she paused, waiting for a sign of encouragement. "What do you think?" she asked finally.

His smile was quick and full of restrained laughter. "I think it sounds like something you've considered carefully for at least ten or fifteen minutes. But I'd suggest you give it at least another five minutes of your imagination before you start tearing out walls."

She frowned at his teasing. "I didn't plan to tear right into it."

"Do you remember the time you had the idea

about the intercom? I had to call in the electrician—"

"Cade, stop teasing." She interrupted his anecdote without hesitation. "I'm serious about this and please refrain from mentioning that I've said that before. I know I have, but it was a long time ago and this is different. I know what I'm talking about. A specialized boutique inside the store could be very profitable. It's certainly worth investigating, don't you think?"

He pushed aside the edges of his jacket and thrust his hands into his trouser pockets. His smile changed to serious contemplation. "I think it's a hell of a risk, Autumn, not to mention the expense and the inconvenience of revamping the store. It would require an enormous outlay of capital, and you couldn't expect to even begin recovering your initial investment for a year or more. Besides that, I'm not sure our customers would be responsive to the idea. Boat supply stores are supposed to sell boat supplies. No one has ever asked for the latest fashion in swimwear."

Autumn blinked at the magnitude of his objections and drew her confidence around her to bolster her resolve. "No one asks, because no one ever thought that a boat supply could offer anything *except* boat supplies. If supermarkets can sell socks and underwear, I know we can sell clothing."

"We?"

The one-word qualification held more discouragement than anything else he'd said. It sank to her toes, taking along her high spirits, but she managed

58

to keep her chin up. "If you don't want to help me, I'll do it on my own."

His mouth tightened impatiently. "It isn't that I don't want to help you, Autumn. I just don't have the time or the energy to finish this kind of major undertaking for you when you tire of it."

Her eyes widened in disbelief and then discouragement fled before a wave of resentment. "I think you'd better apologize for that remark, Cade."

His gaze locked on hers for a seemingly endless, uncomfortable moment. "I'm sorry if I upset you, but I've known you too long to be fooled by a burst of enthusiasm. Over the years you've had dozens of ideas about improving the store and I know for a fact, you never followed through with more than one or two of them. Most of the projects you started either wound up on the back shelf or I finished them for you."

"I was a child, Cade. It isn't fair to make such a generalization."

"Life isn't always fair. I can only go on past experience with you, Autumn, and that tells me that you won't stay around here long enough to see this idea to completion. You'll be chasing rainbows again in no time."

Her breath came hard and fast, forcing her to take a step back from him. She wasn't willing to accept that Cade could actually be saying this to her. "Your faith in me is overwhelming."

Instantly his hand was on her shoulder in a grip that was supposed to soothe, but fell short of its goal. "Now who's being unfair?" he asked. "It has nothing to do with having faith in you. You asked for my opinion and I gave it. I'm not being judgmental, Autumn, I just know you've never been especially happy working here at the store."

The weight of his hand was irritating and she shrugged free, preferring a certain amount of careful distance. "Cade, when I was fifteen I couldn't think of anything except what I might be missing. I'm now twenty-seven and I know I didn't miss anything all those years ago. Responsibility doesn't just happen; it's shaped by experiences. I refuse to apologize to anyone because I had to experience a different type of life before I knew that this is where I belonged."

Cade looked past her, circling the corner of the room with his gaze. "I've never asked for apologies from you, Autumn. I'd just like to see you take your time before making any decision. Once you think about it awhile, you'll see that the boutique idea isn't feasible."

The annoyance she'd thought she had under control blistered a slow path to her tongue, but Cade didn't linger to hear her reaction. Autumn trembled as she watched him walk across the store and into the office. She could never remember being so upset with him. It wasn't fair for him to patronize her like that, to insinuate a feeling of guilt, no matter how small, because she hadn't given the idea careful and thorough consideration before mentioning it to him. He had insulted her with the very words he'd meant to be so wise and understanding. Well, it was about time Cade discovered that he was not her mentor, that she hadn't been asking for his advice, only for his support.

The boutique was a good idea, regardless of how long ago it had occurred to her. She had the experience to get it off the ground and it was feasible. She was willing to bet her savings account on it, and damn it, Cade wasn't going to treat her this way. Autumn followed his line of retreat and whipped past the receptionist's desk without a glance. She pushed on the partially open door of Cade's private office, stepped inside, and closed the door behind her with a defiant click. "I want to know your objections to the boutique, point by point," she announced to his back.

He looked up in surprise, finished taking off his jacket, and hung it on the back of his chair. "I thought I told you."

"No, you based your judgment on the misconception that I wouldn't stay around long enough to finish the project. Well, I am staying, boutique or not, but I want to know why you think it isn't feasible."

Settling himself behind his desk, he picked up a pencil and waved her into a chair across from him, but she remained standing, stubbornly relying on her own strength of purpose.

"First of all," he said evenly if not with a tinge of amusement, "I'm not thrilled with the idea of losing floorspace. I don't like the chaos that comes with remodeling, and I'm not sure I want to sell swimsuits. On a purely business level, I'd have to see the whole thing in black and white, from blueprints to projection sheets."

"Then I'll see that you get the whole thing in black and white."

Cade smiled as if he were proud of this show of spirit on her part. "Maybe you should also get some figures on renting a place of your own for this boutique. Just as a matter of interest."

With cool regard Autumn flatly refused to acknowledge his smile. "You know as well as I do that the overhead costs would be prohibitive. This store is the right place, Cade, and I'll prove it to you . . . on a purely business level. Plus, I don't have to remind you that I own a quarter interest in this store. And although I'm sure you don't believe that I'll stay around to do this, you'll be surprised. You don't know me nearly as well as you think you do." She turned and left his office, ending the discussion with a definitive closing of the door.

With the slam of the office door Cade winced and the pencil he wasn't even aware he held snapped. He hadn't meant to upset her, or maybe he had. He'd certainly intended to discourage her and he'd known with the first words to leave his mouth that he was going about it all wrong.

He stood and walked to the window. Autumn's car was parked on the lot outside. A shiny, black Corvette that irritated him with its flashy newness. Since long before she was old enough to drive she'd wanted a car like it, had told him over and over that one day she'd have one. And now she did.

Somehow as he stared at it, the Corvette took on all the glossy, unreal qualities of the life he imagined she'd enjoyed during the last five years. It was only realistic to believe that she would return to that way of life as surely as she would return at any moment to her car.

Did he want to believe that? Or did he want to be proven wrong? When she presented him with the facts and figures for the boutique, as he was sure that she would, could he evaluate them objectively? Without considering the effect her presence in the store, day after day, might have on him and his resolve to maintain their old relationship?

Whichever way the decision went, it would be unfair to one of them. He could still feel the smallness of her hand tucked trustingly in his, he could still see the eager confidences shining in her eyes. Life was definitely not being fair. With a sigh he turned from the window.

But during the next hour he rose often from his desk to check on the black Corvette. It was almost closing time before the parking space was vacant and Cade wondered where Autumn had gone after slamming out of his office.

He discovered the answer when he went to lock up for the night. She had finished rearranging the display. With the changing of a bulb, she had bathed the window in a new, softer lighting. A sailcloth draped in colorful folds down one side covered the entire display area. It held an eye-pleasing array of odds and ends and couldn't by the wildest stretch of imagination be considered cluttered.

His mouth tightened against the smile that begged for acceptance but that he had to deny. Autumn had drawn the lines of battle without even knowing what was at stake. She had already set out to prove to him that she wasn't a child and in the process she would make their relationship an impossibility.

63

Oh, Autumn, he thought. *I can't let you do it.* He looked at his hand and felt again the warm pressure of her fingertips. *It's too risky . . . too damn risky. And I don't know how in hell to stop you.*

CHAPTER FOUR

A candy-cane-striped awning stretched across a large section of neatly trimmed O'Connor lawn. Beneath the red and white canopy were tables laden with food and drink for the gathering crowd of Eastport residents. Technically the annual Labor Day picnic was for Eastport Marina and Boat Supply employees and their families only, but since almost everyone in town could claim at least a remote kinship to someone who worked there, the picnic had become a community affair. Over the years Autumn had often thought the only thing lacking was a huge banner strung across Eastport's main thoroughfare proclaiming the celebration to all.

Sack races, touch football, even a full-scale Boat Supply versus Marina softball game—all were traditions at the annual picnic. Autumn watched, cheered, participated, and felt as if she had never left home, as if she hadn't missed this event for the past five years. It was only when the activities gave way to serious picnicking that she began to notice the many new faces and the absence of some familiar ones.

As she sat some distance from the canopied area, Autumn nibbled at the food on her plate and tried to remember names and family connections of the employees in her direct line of vision. She wished she had someone close by to assist her faulty memory, but her own family connections, Ross, Lorna, and their offspring, were busily occupied elsewhere. Autumn had barely seen them since the picnic began, and the only other person who might have helped seemed disinclined to come anywhere near her.

Her gaze automatically began to search for Cade, finding him with the ease of long practice. He wasn't so tall that he stood head and shoulders above the crowd, and he wasn't dressed any differently from a dozen others, yet she had no trouble finding him.

He was close enough that she could see the look of serious interest on his face as he spoke to Ray Simpson, the maintenance foreman at the marina. Autumn couldn't hear what they were saying, but she made an educated guess that the two men were talking shop. Cade made a concentrated effort to keep in communication with the employees, and by his own admission he enjoyed the exchange of ideas. It made for a good employer–employee relationship and although Ross made the same effort,

Autumn had always credited Cade with setting the example.

A shining example. That was Cade. Strong, confident, dependable, responsible. She had met many men of varying ages and experience in her years away from Eastport, but not one of them had inspired her respect as Cade did. How had he managed never to reveal a weakness to her? Or had she simply refused to acknowledge that her hero could ever be less than perfect?

With a sigh Autumn bit into a carrot stick and then set her plate aside. Cade wasn't perfect. He took himself too seriously at times, and he lost his temper at least once a month. His life was too structured for her taste, and he preferred his coffee very hot and very black. Not a crucially important list of imperfections, she admitted, but at least it proved she wasn't completely blinded by his good qualities.

Physically it was hard to find fault with him. Out of direct sunlight his hair was a richly textured brown. His features were even and smoothly defined. His shoulders were broad, his stomach flat, his legs lean and long. Autumn frowned. An extra inch in height wouldn't hurt his appearance any, but all-in-all, Cade was—

"Pretty special, isn't he?"

Turning toward the sound, she met dusky eyes framed by thick, black lashes that looked oddly familiar. The delicately feminine brunette placed her cup on the table and seated herself next to Autumn before her dark gaze led the way back to Cade. "He's also the most attractive man here." The soft voice dwindled to a wistful sigh.

Infatuation. Autumn recognized the symptoms and, hiding a smile, she duplicated the sigh. "If only he were a little taller."

"Oh, no. He definitely needs to be a little shorter." The wistful note was replaced by an engaging lilt. "That way he wouldn't be continually knocking down the mistletoe that someone puts over the office door every Christmas."

"And who do you think that *someone* might be? He puts it up every year, then waits for results. But if no one seems to notice . . ." Laughter accented the smile Autumn turned to her companion. "You see? If he were a little taller, he could knock it down without stretching at all when he walked under it."

"I hadn't thought of that." Warm, amiable attention focused on Autumn. "Since we're comparing notes on my boss, I probably should introduce myself. I'm Marilynda Meyers."

Marilynda? This petite, friendly, and fragile-looking woman? Autumn hastily shuffled her preconceived ideas and tried not to show her surprise. "I'm Autumn Tremayne."

"Yes, I know." Marilynda brushed at a peanut-butter smudge on her jeans. "At least I thought you must be. Cade said you'd be the only one with—"

"Don't tell me. I can readily imagine how he described me." Autumn didn't even want to think what he might have said about her. She glanced at Cade with sudden resentment. He hadn't offered *her* even a one-word description of Marilynda. "I should have recognized you right away," she said. "Jay looks very much like you."

The dark eyes softened with maternal pleasure.

68

"Why, thank you. He thinks you look like Firestar. She's one of the cartoon superheroes who save the earth from destruction every Saturday morning, in case you're not acquainted."

"Brian introduced us the first weekend I was home," Autumn said.

"Then you know that Jay meant you only the most sincere compliment." With a casual brush of her fingers Marilynda fluffed her long, wavy hair into becoming disorder. "Sometimes I get distraught when I think that my son is growing up with a cartooned view of the world's problems. But when it's seven o'clock on Saturday morning, I just pull the covers over my head and thank God for those wonderfully farsighted animators. They must all be parents."

It was easy to share an understanding laugh and just as easy to like Marilynda Meyers. Autumn hadn't been prepared for that. But she should have realized Cade would never fall in love with anyone ordinary. And Marilynda was far from ordinary. On a soft, silent sigh, Autumn's lips formed a reluctant curve. "Cade's mentioned you several times, but somehow I pictured you differently."

As Marilynda took a drink from her cup, her dark eyes were quietly appraising. "Cade's mentioned you so often that I'm almost embarrassed to admit you're not quite what I expected either."

Autumn's gaze stole accusingly back to Cade. "I stopped wearing my hair in ponytails and decorating my knees with bandages years ago, but I don't think he's noticed."

"He didn't say a word about ponytails or ban-

69

dages," Marilynda assured with solemn amusement. "But he did say you'd be the only one glowering at him today."

Autumn laughed simply because she hadn't glowered at him even once, but she *had* thought about it. At that moment he looked toward her, smiled, and pulled his hand from his hip pocket to wave. She started to wave back when she realized Marilynda had already done so and that Cade was turning away, apparently satisfied with that response. The laughter suffocated in her throat and Autumn returned her hand to her lap.

"I told him he deserved every glower he got from you," Marilynda continued, "considering what he said about the boutique."

"The boutique?" Autumn echoed, instantly and cautiously alert. "Cade told you about that?"

"Yes." The dark eyes became apologetic. "It wasn't supposed to be a secret, was it?"

Autumn made herself relax. "No, of course not. I'm just surprised he said anything about it. He doesn't think much of the idea."

"Well, I think it's a great idea, Autumn, and I don't understand why Cade objects. My only suggestion would be to elevate the floor in that corner of the room a step or two and add carpeting. That way it will seem more like a store within a store." With a low laugh Marilynda paused. "Needless to say, he wasn't crazy about my idea either, but . . ." The sentence ended on a verbal shrug. "How soon are you going to be able to present him with the facts and figures?"

It was impossible to take offense at such an eager

display of interest and support, yet Autumn recognized the irritation mixed in with the mild pleasure she felt. How could Cade have discussed this with someone else when the idea of the boutique was a point of contention between them? The very thought was annoying and yet she knew the emotion was based more on whom he'd discussed it with than why. She had been right in assuming Marilynda was special to Cade in a way she herself could never be.

"It's going to be another couple of weeks," she answered belatedly. "I'd already thought about adding carpet, but it might be a good idea to raise that section of flooring a step." Autumn hesitated, unsure of what to say next. Her words were going in one direction and her thoughts were scattering in another. "First things first, though. Cade has to come around to our way of thinking."

Marilynda nodded and a thoughtful gleam sparkled in her eyes. "Between the two of us, he doesn't stand a chance. But we won't tell him that." Her smile tilted mischievously. "I'll get Jay to do it."

A disquieting lump lodged in Autumn's throat with the knowledge that Cade's relationship with this mother and son was more than friendly and obviously quite comfortable for all three. She banished the knot of emotion with a cough. "Never underestimate the persuasive power of anyone under twelve," she philosophized in her lightest tone. "Cade has told me he's very fond of Jay. Now if I can get Beth and Brian to take up the cause, Cade will have to surrender."

Autumn raised her brows in cautious amusement.

71

"Does anything about this sound illegal to you? We wouldn't be violating the child-work laws, would we?"

Marilynda again released a low laugh. "I don't know about that, but it's decidedly unfair when three children can accomplish more in one well-timed siege than one adult can do in weeks. And speaking of children, I haven't seen my son in quite a while. Maybe I'd better take a look around." She stood, subjecting the immediate area to a thorough parental scrutiny. With a grimace of resignation she stepped away from the picnic table. "Hide-and-seek," she commented dryly, "my favorite pastime."

Autumn watched Marilynda walk away. A curiously unpleasant sensation trickled down her back when the laughing brunette stopped to exchange an affectionate smile with Cade. What about the search for Jay? Autumn was promptly ashamed of the thought. Marilynda had probably stopped at Cade's request and, more than likely, he would join her in looking for her son. Within moments Autumn watched the two of them move together in the direction of the house.

Together. Cade and Marilynda. He didn't touch the woman beside him in even the most casual way and yet Autumn saw him laugh, saw that secret smile, and felt embarrassingly jealous. In disgust, she rose and tossed the paper plate she had just eaten from into the nearby trash container. Why had she even noticed those special looks that conveyed a sense of togetherness? What was it about a picnic that made her think of sharing secrets and holding hands?

Autumn let the breeze blow her hair. She was perfectly capable of finding someone to hold hands with her if she wanted. After all, somewhere in this crowd she had a niece and nephew who thought she was pretty special too. With a determined frown Autumn started walking toward the noisiest group on the lawn.

It wasn't until the seventh inning of the playoff softball game that Autumn admitted she was trying too hard to enjoy herself. From left field, as she watched the winning run trot home, she decided the whole day had taken too much effort. Or perhaps her heart really hadn't been in it. Whatever the reason, she was tired of the noise, the games, and the crowd.

Even so, she moved in the direction of homeplate to offer congratulations to the players, but detoured abruptly when she saw Cade in the midst of the cheering, noisy group. Marilynda stood at his side and Jay was skipping back and forth in excitement. Ross and Lorna were there, too, ready to hand the traditional trophy to the winning team. Autumn knew they would have made room for her, but she felt oddly displaced in that gathering and she moved quickly away. What had ever made her believe she could slip naturally back into the ebb and flow of Eastport life?

She felt Cade's gaze on her and glanced over her shoulder. His brows were arched in questioning concern, an expression she knew well. He lifted a hand to motion her to join the group, but she shook

73

her head and smiled, just so he'd know she was all right. Otherwise, she thought he might come after her with a bandage, prepared to fix her knee or her spirits, whichever needed attention. He didn't return her gesture, she noticed, and hastened her retreating steps.

That was the problem. She was in need of a smile. Just one. A simple curve of his lips to let her know the rift in their friendship would heal, that their difference of opinion couldn't keep them at odds indefinitely. Maybe that was the root of her low spirits—the fact that she and Cade were still at odds over the boutique idea. They hadn't discussed it further, but she knew it was on his mind by the cool distance he observed whenever she'd been anywhere near, which hadn't been often. Yes, definitely, that must be what was bothering her today.

She reached the conclusion and the boat house at the same time. The dock was shadowed by the gathering twilight and Autumn was grateful the picnic area was on the far side of the house and that no one else had sought a quiet refuge from the noise. She trailed a hand along the sleek sides of Cade's sailboat as her feet traced a slow path over the redwood slats.

Cade hadn't renewed the invitation to sail with him, she thought. Her fingers slid away from the fiberglass hull to brush listlessly against her thigh. She walked to the end of the dock, sat on the edge, and watched the sunset fade to dusk in the water's peaceful reflection. It was familiar and soothing to be alone with the beginning night sounds of the inlet. Growing up hadn't been easy, but this place had helped her gain perspective many times in the past. And she could certainly use some now.

Coming home wasn't what she had thought it would be. There were changes. Confusing changes. But what had actually changed? Not the annual picnic or the basic small-town atmosphere of home. If not what, who, then? Had she changed so much that she couldn't make a place—a grown-up place—for herself here?

Leaning back, Autumn braced herself with her hands and stared at the darkening sky, her thoughts coming full circle to Cade. He'd warned her before she left that nothing stayed the same, but she hadn't believed him. At the time she hadn't really cared. Home had been only a place to leave. Nothing could have persuaded her to stay, and nothing had.

She had spent five years chasing life as though it were something she could capture, as though it were a rare butterfly she could hold in her hand. But each accomplishment, each dream realized, only left her surprised and puzzled by the emptiness in her hands. She had wanted, had planned, so much, but it all seemed sadly unimportant now and she didn't understand why.

Autumn closed her eyes and moved her head in a slow, stretching circle to ease the tight muscles in her neck. It was just today, she reasoned. And the fact that Cade hadn't . . . hadn't what? Talked to her? Smiled at her? Waved? No, it wasn't that. It was the sure knowledge that he was in love with someone else.

Someone else . . . and not her. In slow, devastating comprehension, Autumn opened her eyes. Oh,

God, was she in love with Cade? But how? When? Why hadn't she realized it before now?

Her heart pounded with the unfolding of emotion inside her. Of course she loved him. She'd always adored him. Passionately, intensely, but that was no reason to believe she was in love with him.

But it was. She knew the truth was woven into the very fabric of her life as surely as it was written in the few stars that were visible in the sky above. It had been there all the time, but she hadn't seen, hadn't recognized, the warm, quiet love growing to maturity within her while she was busy chasing butterflies. She was in love with Cade. As simple as that. Simple? What was she thinking? Once, it might have been. But not now. Now her place in his heart, in his life, wasn't secure. Now there was someone else.

"Sulking? Or just telling your troubles to the boat house?" Cade spoke to her from the darkness, his voice as velvet as the night.

Startled, Autumn snapped to attention and she felt a splinter of wood from the dock sting her palm. Panic swirled through her as the stars blurred and then winked in blissful neutrality. They shared her secret, but they offered little sympathy and no advice on how to pretend her feelings for him were the same as they'd always been. Carefully she glanced over her shoulder while concentrating all her emotion on the fragment of discomfort in her palm. "What makes you think I'm sulking?"

"Past experience." He took the few steps necessary to reach her. "You've always come here to sulk when the marina employees lose the softball game. True?"

It would be pointless to deny it. As a resentful adolescent she'd often found even less of an excuse than that for sulking. But she'd outgrown that stage of moodiness long ago. Only Cade still remembered, still insisted on thinking of her as a child.

Autumn sighed. "True," she answered, all the while hoping he would somehow vanish into the realm of her imagination. It was the first time in her memory that she'd truly wished to be alone in preference to being with him. The thought saddened her and made her wish even more for solitude. Gently she touched the tender spot on her palm. "To be honest, I didn't know which team had won. I was just feeling a little crowded, so I came here."

"Mmm." His thoughtful murmur produced a slight frown across her forehead as he sat on the dock beside her. "The crowd does seem noisier than usual, doesn't it?"

"I don't know," she said, trying to ignore the gentle brush of his shoulder against her own. "I've been gone a few years, remember?"

"I remember." Stillness settled between them and lingered a moment too long. "This is like old times, isn't it?" he asked after a while. "We've commiserated over many lost ballgames on this old dock and we've had some pretty hefty disagreements here, too, haven't we?"

Autumn sent him a wry, sideways glance. "Some of them were almost as hefty as the disagreement we're now having over my ideas for the store."

He grimaced and looked away. "Just like old

times—right down to the familiar feeling that you're getting ready to start an argument."

Why did he have to sit so close to her? And why didn't she simply scoot over and give herself some much-needed space? "I'm not in the mood for arguments or disagreements tonight," she said. "Especially about the boutique."

"Good." He sounded genuinely relieved and Autumn watched in surprise as he jumped lightly to his feet and walked to the sailboat. "I had a hell of a time getting these down here without a calamity," he explained as the clink of fine crystal chimed softly in the air. "And I set them on the boat deck until I could—test the waters, so to speak. I didn't want to waste good champagne if you were dead set on arguing."

He was back beside her within seconds, leaning down to hand her a glass. "Be careful not to spill it," he cautioned as she tentatively accepted his offering. "This is a rare peacemaking wine from my own private cellar. It's not to be confused with the many imitations you see on supermarket shelves, and please never refer to it as ordinary champagne. It may look the same, but don't be fooled. This wine has a mission." Again he sat close beside her and held his glass up to the moonlight.

Silvery bubbles diffused the light into a prism of color and her throat ached with emotion. How was it possible to suddenly love him more than she already did? Her eyes were drawn to his face, but when he turned to her, she turned away, knowing her only protection lay in pretense. "Does that mean this wine has a 'high' purpose?"

78

His aggrieved gaze was quick and to the point. "That was unworthy of you, Autumn. Try to concentrate, would you?"

"Right." She raised the glass to her lips, but he stopped her.

"That wasn't what I meant by concentrating," he interrupted. "You can't take a drink until we've made peace."

"Oh." Eyeing him doubtfully, she lowered the glass. "You're doing this backward, Cade. I'll feel much more peaceful *after* I drink the wine."

"This isn't working. I followed you for the sole purpose of suggesting a truce, or at least a moratorium on the subject of the boutique. If you protested, I intended to ply you with wine until you agreed."

"No plying is necessary. I hereby agree to a ceasefire," she stated firmly. "Said cease-fire will go into effect at once and last until all sales data are gathered, at which time open combat will resume."

His laugh was throaty. "I'll drink to that." He brought his glass against hers in a sedate toast, then took it to his lips.

Autumn followed his movements with eyes that were helpless to look elsewhere. His mouth curved along the rim of the crystal and as he sipped, she imagined the cool effervescent wine clinging to his lips and coming to hers in a lingering kiss.

This was Cade, who had sat with her on this dock more times than she could remember; Cade, who had comforted her when she'd failed to win the valentine of her choice in fifth grade; Cade, who had often understood her better than she had herself. But he wouldn't understand this. Autumn took a drink and then another, swallowing quickly in hopes the wine would dull the razor-sharp edge of her tension. She was breathlessly aware of the man beside her, painfully conscious of the betraying ache in her stomach.

The desire to touch him was as real as the splinter under her skin. Yet she knew the tiny splinter could be removed easily, while the need to kiss him, caress him, and know the beauty of loving him as a woman would never leave her. The silence between them was unobtrusive. It was the soft sharing she had enjoyed with Cade, but now it seemed rough with confusing emotions. How swiftly everything could change.

"I met Marilynda." The thought came from nowhere and was spoken before she realized her intention. "She's very lovely. And nice. I liked her right away." Frowning, Autumn slowed the momentum of the words and sipped at her wine. "I can see why you think she's pretty special."

He turned in her direction with a slow, guarded look. "Can you, Autumn?"

"Well, yes," she said hesitantly. "Marilynda is— Oh, I don't know. She just seems somehow *suited* to you."

"Suited?" he repeated, and raised his glass to drain the remainder of his wine in one swallow. "So you're already making plans to give the groom away."

"No! I couldn't—" Autumn stopped and deliberately softened the denial with a constrained laugh. "You're not mine to give away."

80

"No." He was silent then, until he broke the mood as he set down his wineglass and said, "Tell me about living in New York. Was it all you expected it to be? Do you miss it?"

The splinter bit a little deeper into her palm as she clenched her hand. Why had he changed the subject? Why wouldn't he tell her about Marilynda? God, why did she even want to know?

"New York is"—she paused to give herself time to consider—"exhilarating, exhausting. It's so much more than I imagined, but I'm not sure it's all that I expected. I loved living there—except when I hated it. Maybe I just didn't belong."

No, she had never belonged there. She knew that now. Her heart had been restless, searching for home, for Cade.

"It's very different from Eastport."

"Yes."

"Are you going back?"

"No! Cade, I told you I'm home to stay. I'm not saying there won't be a few adjustments to make, but I'm staying here."

He laughed softly and warmed her with a smile. "Touchy, aren't you? I was only asking if you're going back for a visit sometime."

That wasn't what he'd meant. It had been another way of challenging her, and Autumn refused to reply. From the corner of her eye she saw the deepening of his grin and knew he was not going to drop the subject entirely.

"How many broken hearts did you leave behind?" His voice followed the amused curve of his lips. "Dozens?"

"Oh, at least that many." She thought that if nothing else she could match his teasing tone. "None, however, that won't mend."

"You don't really expect me to believe that. Surely you left one that's beyond repair . . . or maybe *your* heart is the one in need of fixing." His shoulder bumped hers as he shifted position and unexpectedly lifted her hand from her lap to cradle it, palm up, in his own. "Does your heart still belong to you, Autumn? Or did you lose it somewhere on the other side of the horizon?"

Her trembling began with his first touch and intensified with his words. What could she say? The discovery of her love for him was too recent to deny, too new to confess. She needed to think. She needed time to adjust. She needed to get her hand away from his.

"Don't do that," she said, jerking her hand from his light grasp. She felt foolish then for making her emotional discomfort so obvious. An explanation, however lame, seemed unavoidable. "I—I have a splinter."

"I'm sorry. Here, let me look." His concern was instant and honest and before she had a chance to explain further, her hand was back in his. If she protested his concern, she'd either hurt her hand or his feelings, so Autumn allowed herself to feel the tenderness of his touch against her skin.

"Hmmm," he murmured, "can't see a thing, but if you think surgery is necessary, I could get a flashlight from—"

"No, thank you, Dr. Frankenstein. I'll tough it out." She began to pull her hand free, but his fingers closed over hers and wouldn't release her. Her eyes sought his in the twilight as he slowly raised her palm to his lips. His kiss lingered longer than a heartbeat, but not nearly as long as she might have wished. "There," he said as he placed her hand back in her lap, "that should speed your recovery. Sorry I don't have a bandage."

Autumn couldn't have made a reply even if she'd wanted to do so, and the ensuing silence was welcome. Her whole body trembled with his nearness; her palm tingled. For her his kiss had been a moment of devastating awareness; for him it had been a moment of kiss-it-and-make-it-well comfort. What a difference loving made.

"Tell me about Richard."

Oh, no. She wasn't about to get into another discussion of "boyfriends." "There's nothing to tell," she said. She sensed Cade's half-irritated smile, but kept her gaze on the ripple of reflected stars in the water.

"You always said you intended to fall in love with a wealthy man."

"I've said a lot of foolish things."

"Did you fall in love with Richard?"

"What difference does it—" Autumn broke off the protest. Why not tell him the extent of her foolishness? It would give him the chance to say "I told you so." "Yes, at least I thought I was in love with him." Her memory winged back to the days when love was a bouquet of exotic flowers or flying to St. Thomas for lunch. Oh, she had been in love all right, but not with Richard. He only represented the lifestyle she'd dreamed of having. Fortunately she'd realized her mistake before the never-serious Richard began to think seriously. That time in her life had been foolish and flighty and fun, and she wouldn't trade it for anything—except perhaps a change of heart.

Cade moved beside her and her thoughts came home. "Richard is a wonderful man." She summed up her feelings in a sentence. "But he never quite measured up to my idea of a hero."

"Ordinary men seldom do." The words were low and oddly sad.

Autumn felt a familiar need to tease away any hint of sadness. "Don't you think I deserve a little better than ordinary?"

His reply was long in coming and so soft, she wondered at its huskiness. "I've always thought you deserved the best, Autumn."

Tension closed over her as she recognized his stillness and she turned to him impulsively. "Cade?"

Their eyes met and held as reason shattered around her. She leaned forward and brushed his mouth with her own, but the touch was inadequate. Desire welled and spilled over onto her lips and she gave in to her love for him. Her breasts pushed against her T-shirt, seeking and finding stimulation against his muscled chest. She leaned on him for support and let her arms move around his shoulders until her fingers found the hair at his nape.

She ignored his cautious response, allowing him little room for retreat, and then his arms were sliding around her, holding her as he began to take charge of the caress she'd initiated. In all her daydreams she'd never dreamed of a kiss that was fulfilling and frightening all at once. She was eager to be closer, to experience more of him, but she was afraid of feeling too much, of giving more than she could afford to lose.

Her pulsing emotions swirled into warm curls of need. He parted her lips with a fiercely daring gentleness and Autumn responded with a passion newly discovered and all her own. But, abruptly, the kiss ended and his hands were gripping her shoulders, propelling her back, away from him.

"Autumn!" The raspy calling of her name penetrated her consciousness slowly and it took a full minute before she comprehended the angry note in his voice. What had she done? That was not the sort of kiss exchanged between friends, and Cade had been totally unprepared for her sudden impulsive embrace. She should have thought; she should have realized . . .

With an unsuccessful attempt to smile, Autumn stood and took a wary step back and then another. "Good night, Cade." It was amazing that she could sound so casual. Astounding that she could turn and walk away as if she didn't want to run madly to safety. She heard the impatient echo of his steps behind her and knew he wasn't going to let her escape.

"Autumn." He caught her arm and pulled her to face him, his height intimidating and emphasized by the dusky light. "I don't want that to happen again."

She took a deep breath. "It was only a ki—"

"I *know* what it was!" His grip tightened. "And I don't want you to do it again."

"You have no reason to be so self-righteous, Cade. It was *just* a kiss and I did have your complete cooperation, didn't I?"

His anger was becoming a tangible part of the atmosphere. "A veneer of sophistication doesn't mean you've grown up, Autumn. You're still a child, running home to bandage a broken heart. I recognize all the classic symptoms, but I'm not going to play nursemaid this time. And I'm not about to become a testing ground for your wounded femininity. Be careful, Autumn, about backing friendship into a corner!" He released her and took a step away.

But now it was her turn to stop him. Her fingers closed on his muscular forearm. "And *you* be careful, Cade, of thinking I'm still a child. No matter how you feel about it, sooner or later you'll have to accept the fact that children grow up. And I have, Cade. I have."

She felt the tension in his arm flex beneath her touch. Slowly she brought her hand back to her side, only then realizing the ache in her palm. The splinter had burrowed deeper with the pressure and Autumn soothed it with a gentle massage, but her gaze never dropped from Cade's. Even when he turned his back and walked from her sight, she continued to stare.

"I love you," she whispered, knowing and accepting that there would never be an answer. Only the stars would know and someday the soft hurt

86

inside her would be as insignificant as the splinter under her skin.

But he had kissed her, her heart reminded her. Really kissed her. Autumn sighed wistfully. Yes, he had, and somehow the memory took away the sting —from her hand and from her heart.

CHAPTER FIVE

Autumn approached Cade's office door with an armload of paper ammunition, one exorbitantly expensive bottle of wine, more than a touch of trepidation, and Marilynda's insistent encouragement. In fact, the entire office staff was offering supportive smiles as Autumn walked past.

It was nice to know the employees were behind her, but not so nice when she considered that their support placed her opposite Cade in an employer-versus-employer battle. She didn't want that. No matter how much she believed in her idea and her ability to make it successful, she wouldn't pursue it without his agreement. She trusted his judgment, knew he would be fair, and she admitted to herself that his support was the only one that counted.

Even if she'd owned half of the corporation instead of a fourth, she wouldn't do it. Mainly because she couldn't bear to be always at odds with him.

And yet she wasn't sure she could manage the close contact the project would require either. It was a catch-22; she had to stay and prove to him that she had learned responsibility; but if she stayed, knowing she loved him, sooner or later she was bound to act irresponsibly. As she had on the boat dock after the champagne . . .

Stopping in front of the closed door, Autumn took a deep breath and cautiously adjusted the materials in her arms as she waited for assistance. Marilynda, looking as managerial as if she had an Office Manager badge on her jacket, stepped forward and opened the door. "Mr. O'Connor," she said in a supremely businesslike voice, "your two o'clock appointment is here." She stood back as Autumn moved into the office, then closed the door with a whispered, "Go get him, tiger."

Autumn hesitated as Cade rose to stand behind his desk. Trepidation vanished beneath the curiously uneven throbbing of her pulse. Why had she thought he should be taller? He looked wonderfully free of faults, all the way from the soft cashmere sweater worn over a crisp oxford shirt to his dark gray slacks to the carefree style of his hair to his indigo eyes. The corner of his mouth held the promise of laughter, but he regarded her with perfect seriousness. He made no move to come around his desk and help her with the load she carried. The amused arch of his brows brought up Autumn's confidence and she stepped forward to let everything slide from her arms onto the desktop. At that unexpected gesture Cade did move.

He caught the bottle of wine just as it rolled over

89

the edge of the desk. After a quick examination he placed it upright and nodded appreciatively. "This is beginning to look like a royal setup. Is the bottle a bribe or just a means to impede my judgment?"

With growing self-assurance Autumn sank onto the upholstered office chair across from him. "It's for celebrating our new business venture . . . or for breaking over your head, if necessary."

He returned to his chair and leaned back before giving her a deliciously lazy grin. "Hello, Autumn."

She could have basked for days in the silky resonance of his voice and the easy sensuality in his eyes, but she simply melted a little farther into her chair. "Hello, Cade."

"So you're the mysterious two o'clock appointment. Marilynda's been flitting in and out of here all day as if she thought I might try to escape through the window. She seems to have rallied quite a bit of support for your boutique."

"It serves you right, Cade, for talking out of school in the first place. This will only make it harder for you to turn me down."

The laugh lines around his mouth deepened into a pensive smile. "I've always found it next to impossible to refuse you anything, Autumn, and I'm sure this will be no exception. Besides, it isn't up to me to give a flat yes or no. You and Ross have as much to say about it as I do."

"You know Ross would never take my side against you, if it ever came to that. He's my brother and I love him, but he wouldn't hesitate to pool his quarter interest with yours any day. All you have to do is express your doubts and Ross will fall right in line."

"It serves you right, Autumn, for leaving us to manage everything for you while you were off living the life of luxur—"

"I think perhaps now is the time to *break* open the wine," she interrupted sweetly.

He laughed and leaned forward. "That won't be necessary. I'm nothing if not flexible. Let's see what you've got here." He picked up the top few information sheets and began to read.

Autumn started to explain the basis for her profit and loss projections, but decided to give him a little time to examine them first. Nervously she watched his forehead crease in concentration. She ran her palm over her navy slacks, adjusted the cuff of her matching blazer, and stopped short of rearranging the silk bow tied at the collar of her blouse. Her finger tangled with a coppery curl at her neck as she tried not to ask what he thought so far.

"Do you have an estimate on the remodeling costs?" he asked abruptly, and Autumn jumped to attention. She rose to bend over the desk and find the estimates he wanted.

"Here." She handed him two preliminary bids, but remained standing as he looked at them. "I have the preliminary drawings too." Without waiting for his answer she withdrew the first sketch from its protective tube and spread it open on his desk. "Marilynda suggested putting the boutique on a platform to give the illusion of separate stores, so there's one sketch with that option and one without."

She reached for the cardboard tube containing the other sketch. Cade also reached for the tube

91

and her hand closed over his, bringing her heart to her throat in one swift leap. Large, rough, and warm, he felt intoxicatingly male and Autumn lost all rational thought for that electric instant. In slow motion she drew back, allowing him to get the drawing and spread it out on top of the other. Carefully avoiding his eyes, she tried to look totally absorbed as she frantically sought to remember what she'd been saying.

Cade watched her with curious surprise. It wasn't like Autumn to be nervous, especially with him. But her hand had trembled when she'd accidentally touched him just now. He wasn't mistaken about that and yet he didn't understand it either. Maybe he'd underestimated the importance she placed on this project. Maybe it really did matter to her. She'd certainly done a thorough job on getting everything in black and white. That in itself surprised him, but not nearly as much as her odd tremor.

Now, if it had been his hand that shook at her touch, he wouldn't have wondered. But he'd long ago steeled himself against Autumn's impulsive embraces and he thought he'd done a damn good job of being impersonal in his responses. Until the kiss on the dock. That had been almost three weeks ago, but still he ached with the memory. And she had been so casual, so blasé—*it was only a kiss,* she'd said. *Only a kiss.* She just didn't know.

As she began to explain the renovation plans in detail, he told himself he must listen carefully. He owed her his full attention, but somehow she'd managed to throw his power of concentration off balance. She was so slender, her body softly curved and alluring. Her hair reflected the warm colors of a cozy fire and her creamy skin practically begged a caress.

Don't be a fool! he commanded himself even as he moved around the desk to be near her. He wondered if she really tensed at his approach or if he only imagined it. She didn't look at him as she continued pointing out the benefits of opening a boutique inside the boat supply store. He stayed close beside her and looked intently at each data sheet she put before him. Occasionally she brushed against him, and each time he was reminded of how fragile the threads of their friendship actually were. He could lose her trust, her affection, her innocent belief in heroes, in one unguarded moment.

"Well," she asked in a low but hopeful voice. "What do you think?"

I think I love you. Cade walked away from the admission and away from Autumn. How could he expect to work in close association with her for months into the future if he couldn't even make it through the initial presentation? Safely behind his desk, he absently shuffled through her carefully gathered information. She had done exactly as he'd asked. She'd presented her idea in concise black and white and he was beginning to feel the unyielding wall at his back.

"I think you've presented a convincing case, Autumn. To be honest, I still have some reservations, but I have to agree that the idea seems feasible. What are you planning to do about financing?"

Breathing a tiny sigh of relief, she told him the amount of capital she had to invest and that Richard

Colburn had agreed to finance the balance. Cade's eyes grew frosty blue at that, she noted.

"I'll finance the balance, Autumn. I don't want outsiders in this store."

"But, Cade," she said, ready to defend her choice of investors, "it will be strictly for the boutique and—"

"*I'll* do it. And if you were planning to use your interest in the corporation as collateral on a loan with Colburn, I *don't* want to know. Just don't even think about doing that." He ran his fingers through the dusky hair at his temples, leaving it disheveled and appealing. "Please, Autumn, just humor me on this."

Autumn sank back to the edge of her chair, half afraid to believe he was actually going to capitulate without a struggle.

Rubbing a hand along his jaw, Cade sorted through the projection sheets once more before he looked at her again. "Have you talked to James Clayton at the bank? You'll need a line of credit, you know, before you can order the merchandise you want."

Of course she knew, and the fact that he thought it necessary to remind her was irritating somehow. "I'm sure that won't be any problem."

"Then you've talked to James?"

"No, but I'm positive he'll agree. After all, he's handled the corporation finances for years."

Cade was openly skeptical. "He's also the banker who used to help you unravel your personal finances every few months."

"That was years ago, Cade!" Autumn sat forward,

her mouth forming a tight line as her irritation grew.

"Which is another thing to consider," he stated calmly. "You've lived away from Eastport for several years. Banks tend to take that into account when approving credit. However, I suppose I could—"

"No. I'll take care of this myself."

"All right, Autumn. Why don't you get back to me on this after you speak to James." His smile was firm. "I'd really prefer that you use the local bank."

"Then that's what I'll do." She kept her tone even although she couldn't keep her foot from tapping a rhythm of aggravation. Damn! Why hadn't she checked on the line of credit? Because she hadn't believed it would be any problem . . . and it wouldn't be either. Still, Cade didn't have to look so pleased about the delay in giving her a definite yes.

Autumn began to gather her pieces of paper into order even as she restored order to her disposition. It wasn't Cade's fault that she had neglected this one legitimate question. She had known, of course, that she would need an agreement with the bank. All clothing stores required an open-ended type of borrowing in order to purchase from the manufacturer, sell to the public, and repay the loan before starting the whole process over again. She knew the routine; she just had never started from the very beginning before.

When everything was neatly stacked and the blueprints replaced in their tubes, she eyed the wine bottle. "I don't suppose it would be appropriate to celebrate our new business venture just yet, would it?"

Cade shook his head in apology. "I'm afraid it would be premature. However, if you'd consider offering me a bribe—"

"I could get in a lot of trouble by offering you something like that. You might think I had no integrity. You might even refuse to share the wine with me."

"Try me and see," he coaxed with a smile, and Autumn thought she would have given him much more than the wine for that smile.

She took the bottle and handed it to him. "Forget integrity. After all that talking I would love to have a drink."

With a look of mock disapproval, Cade accepted the wine and placed the bottle securely out of reach on the bookshelf behind his desk. "No intoxicating beverages allowed during working hours, Autumn. You know the rules."

"Cade! I knew I should have gone with my first instincts."

"But think what you would have missed."

The laughter in his eyes was addictive, but she managed to resist. "The pleasure of breaking it over your stubborn—"

"No, the pleasure of my company at dinner."

"Dinner?" she echoed. "Tonight?"

"Unless you have other plans?"

"No." She knew she probably should refuse, but Cade would think that very odd. "I'd like that."

"So would I," he said. "It's September twenty-second, Autumn. Your special day. Did you think I would forget?"

The first day of autumn. The day Cade had long since decreed belonged especially to her. The day he'd always managed to make special in so many different ways. It had been a long time since she'd been here to share it with him. Had he thought of her on those days past? Would he think of her on this day in the future?

"To be honest, Cade, I'm the one who forgot." Why did her voice sound so listless? And why did his eyes seem suddenly a weary blue? In a distant corner of memory she saw Cade tuck a sunflower into her ponytail and her own self-important pleasure. *You can be the sun in my mornings, Autumn. Your hair's certainly bright enough.* His remembered words brought a reminiscent curve to lips that no longer pouted at his teasing, but still knew how to win his smile. "I am free this evening, however . . . in case you're having a party for me, I do have a few names you might want to add to the guest list—no more than two hundred or so—but you'll have plenty of time if you start right away." She paused to watch the betraying crease at the side of his mouth. "Last-minute get-togethers are so much fun, don't you think?"

His lips tightened with resistance before giving in to the smile. "Be ready at seven, Autumn. We'll have just the kind of party you like."

"Party of two," Cade told the hostess at Whitecliffs.

As far as Autumn could tell, the restaurant's only

97

pretension to elegance was its name. There were no hanging baskets of flowers to suggest a hidden garden, no candlelight to dance upon mirrored reflections—possibly because there were no mirrors. The view from the windows was dark, but she graciously assumed that it would be a very nice view during the daytime. The tables were cloth-covered and the matching napkins were folded neatly beneath silverware that was shiny, but a long way from the rich gleam of sterling.

After the hostess had left them with menus and the promise of coffee, Autumn leaned forward. "So this is Eastport's newest eating establishment. It's impressive compared to Bernie's, isn't it?"

Cade lowered his menu. "Almost anything is impressive if compared to Bernie's. The decor there is a neon sign out front and a hand-printed bill of fare over the door. The food is good though. But wait until you taste the seafood here, Autumn. It more than makes up for the lack of stiff-necked maître d's and glitzy decor you're used to."

With a blink of surprise Autumn laid her menu on the table. "Why would anyone *want* to become used to that?"

"Don't ask me. You're the one who always said atmosphere was the most important part of 'dining.'"

There was a glimmer of challenge in the blue eyes regarding her and a hint of cool irritation in the look she returned. "I was wrong. The most important part is enjoying the company of the person across the table."

The corner of his mouth slanted slowly upward. "Then you and I are in luck tonight, aren't we?"

Two steaming cups provided by a pleasant waitress took the place of a reply and Autumn concentrated on adding cream to her coffee. She didn't feel especially lucky. Or even very special. From the moment she'd floated down the stairs, ready to spend the evening or the rest of her life with him, Cade had dampened her spirits with the most innocuous of remarks.

You look nice, he had said, wiping out in three words the extra time and effort she'd spent on her appearance. *Watch your skirt,* had been his only comment on her teal blue off-the-shoulder, far too expensive afternoon dress. She had bought it in Paris on impulse, using close to an entire month's salary, and Cade had almost shut the car door on it. He would have, too, if she hadn't quickly gathered in the circle skirt at his command. *You should have brought a sweater,* was as close as he came to noticing what she considered a very flattering neckline. He hadn't wasted any time on getting to Whitecliffs restaurant either, and Autumn had been tempted to ask if he had a late date.

She hadn't asked though. How could she explain that she wanted him to notice her, to appreciate her femininity . . . to love her? How long could she pretend she loved him as nothing more than a friend? How long before he realized something had changed? Cade was still the same companion he'd always been to her, but that was an elusive comfort. She was no longer the same and that made everything he did, every word he said, different.

99

Aware of the amused silence at their table, she glanced up to meet his smile. "If you stir that anymore, Autumn, you'll have butter instead of cream in your coffee."

She placed the spoon on the saucer and raised her russet eyebrows in guilty concession.

"Daydreaming?" he asked gently.

"Just thinking."

"About me?"

There were so many things she would have liked to say at that moment, so many things that would forever go unsaid. With a soft, wistful laugh she shook her head. "I was thinking about restaurants and atmosphere—and how lucky I am to be here with you on the first day of fall." She picked up her menu. "I'm starving. What should I order?"

From that point on the evening passed in comfortable enjoyment. The food was as good as Cade's promise, but Autumn knew it was his charm, his ability to make her feel special in an ordinary world, that left the pleasurable taste. It took only a casual suggestion to persuade him that a leisurely drive would be a nice way to waste an hour.

He teased her when she began to yawn halfway through the hour. But Autumn had no intention of falling asleep and losing even a moment of the memories she was storing like handfuls of sunshine for a rainy day. She didn't mean to let the conversation drift into companionable silence and she didn't mean to close her eyes—not for a second—but it was so comfortable.

As the bronze strands of her hair brushed his shoulder, Cade took a deep, controlled breath and thought, *Stay awake, Autumn*. But in a glance he knew she was already asleep. With a carefully quiet sigh he put his arm around her and let her nestle against his side. He drove home and parked the car in his drive, thinking that he could walk Autumn home across the lawn in a few minutes—thinking anything to keep from thinking how good it felt to have her next to him.

The outside light cast a soft glow on the shadowy interior of the car, subduing color and basking Autumn's vibrant energy in dusky sleep. Cade allowed himself the luxury of admiring her—a longing he'd denied all evening—and let his gaze touch her at will. A subtle fragrance tantalized him and he wanted badly to investigate the creamy expanse of her shoulder and discover the hidden scent. But he didn't dare.

A throaty hum parted her lips and tenderness closed around his heart. She was content to be with him, awake or dreaming, and he was glad. With one hand tucked beneath her cheek, she looked sweetly innocent, but there, in the dark fringe of lashes, along the curve of her chin, in the seductive fullness of her lower lip . . . he could see the sensuality, the untapped passion for life and love that was uniquely hers. The passion he wanted to claim for his own. But he didn't dare.

She stirred, curving one leg back to rest on the seat. The hem of her skirt slipped above her knee to reveal a slim thigh that tapered to a shapely calf and ankle. Her shoe, a lacy network of leather, hung loosely, half on, half off her slender foot. His gaze lingered along that foot as he warned himself to awaken her, to take her home, to put her safely beyond his reach. Each moment only served to make him more aware of the moments he couldn't share with her. Each casual touch made him realize he was far from being the strong, invulnerable hero Autumn thought him to be.

He followed the path of light and shadow past the contours of her leg to the shimmering blue fabric that denied him further passage. *Isn't this a beautiful dress, Cade?* she had asked him on some long-forgotten yesterday as she spun in slow circles for his approval. *Do you think he will like it?*

Cade had assured her that any he would have to be blind not to like it. As for himself, he had seldom paid that much attention to what she wore, not while she was still girlish enough to ask his opinion. He had answered her questions absently, never thinking that one day she would drift down the stairs in a dress that left him speechless, left him wanting to tell her she looked beautiful, but unable to do so. Anything more than the simple compliment he had finally managed to give would have confused her. And then he would have had to explain, somehow . . . and he didn't dare.

To brush the tendrils of hair at her temple with his fingertips, to place a whisper-soft kiss against one red-gold curl, that was all he dared, for now, for ever. No. He knew better. The moment of reckoning would come. Autumn would see the truth in his eyes someday and then, Lord only knew what he would dare.

"Autumn?" He called to her gently, knowing that

he must wake her before he grew even more vulnerable to the feel of her in his arms. "Autumn."

There was no response except for a slight change in the rhythm of her breathing. He leaned closer to her ear, automatically concealing his longing behind a façade of amusement. "Wake up, Autumn. Don't you remember? You're the one who wanted to dance every night until dawn, you're the one who said you came alive in the nighttime. Were you only teasing me all those years ago, Autumn? Is there a magic spell to release the dancing fool in you?"

Heavy lashes made a lingering sweep across her cheek before rising upward. She moved, tilting her head back against his arm to look at him in drowsy question. "Cade?" she whispered. "I was dreaming. I was in a field of"—her voice faded sleepily—"of sunflowers and you were there too." Her eyelids lowered, then slowly opened again. "Don't tease me anymore, Cade. I'm too old to wear sunflowers in my hair."

He smiled at the nonsensical request and held her as he waited for her to come fully awake. "I won't tease you, Autumn," he answered solemnly. "And I won't ask you to wear sun—" She was moving against him, her arms winding their way around his neck, pulling his head down, breathing his name in a husky, dreamy murmur. Before he had time to react, he knew the time for denial had already passed. Her lips were caressing his, following the outline of his mouth from one corner to the other. Her breath was warm, seductive; her body was softly yielding; her fingers were a tantalizing pressure at his nape. His will was nonexistent.

"What are you trying to do to me, Autumn?" He heard the hoarse quality of his whisper, but knew only the tender texture of her lips. Drowning. This must be the way it felt to drown, to spin in circles of knowing it couldn't be happening, that any moment you would begin to resist, to save yourself. But he had no desire to be saved. His arms tightened around her as the kiss wove through his thoughts with sensuous persuasion.

Her mouth opened at his cue and it was his turn to caress the feminine contour of her lips. A tremor of sound vibrated against him and he felt his body respond. Gentle hands slid to her hips and pulled her closer, cradling her against his thigh. His fingers traced the satiny pattern of her dress, exploring the shape beneath the material. He hesitated when his knuckles brushed the slope of her breast, but with slight pressure, she pulled him deeper into the kiss and his palm covered the tautness that seemed to strain toward him.

He eased his mouth away from hers to discover the silken creaminess of her cheek, to find the delicate shell of her ear, and then to follow the curve of her shoulder. His heartbeat was an audible rhythm that echoed through him with each new delight. She was so lovely, so beautifully formed, and he wanted to intimately know more of her. His lips etched feathery circles on her bare skin and dipped lower to the inviting smoothness just below the neckline of her dress.

Deftly his hand went to her back and released the

single fastening that held the neckline in place. He paused then, returning to her lips to claim her agreement. She clung to him, her acceptance, her willingness evident in the fierce emotion of her kiss. When he touched her, his fingers light and tender against her breast, she trembled and a low moan escaped her.

With the sound, Cade was suddenly aware that he was not drowning, that he could stop this wonderful, sensual irresponsibility if he wanted. But he didn't want to stop. He didn't want to think clearly. He didn't want to realize that he was holding Autumn, touching her, kissing her. She offered no resistance; she seemed eager to share his desire, so why should he be the one to say no? He had wanted her for so long, but even with the thought, he lessened the intensity of their embrace. This was Autumn, who, in a few moments, would look at him if not accusingly, at least with eyes shadowed and dark with questions. He had protected her emotions too long and he couldn't violate her trust any further. His hand moved from her breast, but before he replaced the material, he knew he couldn't stop just yet. Slowly his lips left hers and he bent his head to sip at her rosy sweetness.

Her stillness conveyed that Autumn, too, was suddenly aware and he leisurely drew back, sliding her dress into place and fastening it as unobtrusively as he could. When he risked a glance at her, he felt his throat close in a tense knot. Her head was bent, but her arms still encircled him, her hands resting at his shoulders. A deep sigh began low in his chest and was trapped in his lungs as he held her to his side until her breathing slowed and the unnatural stiffness eased a little. He had to say something, had to make her understand.

Logic balked at that point. He didn't understand what had just happened between them . . . or perhaps he did. Autumn had been asleep, dreaming of things he knew nothing of, and he had taken advantage of her dreams. Her impulsive kiss had been just that, an impulse that he should have gently but firmly rejected.

She moved, drawing away from his hold, and this time he let her go. He felt the distance that settled between them, although she hadn't physically moved far.

"You need to be more careful with those impulses," he said thickly, but with what he hoped was a touch of his usual steadiness. "That one almost got us into more trouble than I could handle." He felt the wounded look she turned to him, but forced himself not to see. "I know that you've been used to a different lifestyle, Autumn, but you're home now. You can't exchange kisses as casually as a handshake anymore, at least not here. You were with me and still things got out of hand. Demonstrations like that test even my control, Autumn, so I hope you'll be more careful in the future." God! He sounded like a damned self-righteous hypocrite. Whom was he kidding? No one except Autumn and maybe that was the reason for such a godawful speech. She was angry. He felt the tension in her strict posture, saw the stubborn angle of her chin.

"You can *count* on that, Cade. From now on I'll be

very careful about my impulses, but you might want to be more selective about your *demonstrations*. If an impulse can test your control, you should be very careful about the company you keep." With that, Autumn was sliding across the seat and getting out of the car. Giving the door a definitive slam, she walked automatically toward the gap in the hedge between her home and Cade's, defying him to follow her by the rigid set of her shoulders.

He didn't even try to follow, and in a few minutes the night air had cooled her burst of temper, but had done nothing for the aching need inside her. She had been impulsive. She had awakened in his arms and it had seemed natural to stay there. She had wanted to kiss him, and kiss him she had. Her body stirred with the memory of his touch, the feel of his hands.

The hedge caught at her dress as she walked past. The material puckered despite her efforts to work it free without ruining her once-in-a-lifetime dress. It had been irresponsible to wear it in the first place, but she'd wanted to show Cade . . . what? That she was grown-up? The very thought made it childish. But Cade's actions were no better than her own, and she wouldn't forgive him any too soon for making that comment about demonstrations. If she weren't so desperately lost in loving him, she might just demonstrate some of her other impulses. But she was and she wouldn't.

Frowning her displeasure with life in general, Autumn broke the twig that held her prisoner, even though she knew she would never get it out without tearing the fabric. It seemed fitting, somehow, that she now had a legitimate reason for never wearing the dress again.

CHAPTER SIX

"Autumn, could I see you in my office, please?"

Autumn looked up, balancing herself with her
hand on the lower shelf railing. Cade stood at the
end of the store aisle, one side of his dark tweed
jacket drawn back by the hand resting easily in his
trouser pocket. The knot in his navy tie was as polished as the shine on his black leather shoes, and his
oxford shirt was impressively white. Her breath
made a quivery attempt to hold steady, but her
heartbeat made no such effort.

For almost two weeks it had been the same. Every time she saw him, across the room or nearby,
she felt the same tremulous sensations, remembered the taste of his lips, the touch of his hand.
Even now her breasts throbbed with the memory.
But she would pretend she didn't remember, that
she didn't care. It was becoming a real challenge to

pretend that nothing had happened, but Cade had set the guidelines by his own strict behavior.

"Autumn." His voice, crisp and businesslike, broke into her thoughts and commanded her attention.

Reluctantly she met his gaze and thought that he didn't need to make such a point of standing a careful distance away. If he'd stood right beside her, the distance between them wouldn't have been any less obvious. With a sigh she stood up and half expected him to take a step back.

"I'd like to talk to you, please," he stated in the same crisp tones. "In my office. In five minutes if that's all right."

He didn't need to make such a point of being polite either. "Let's make it now," she said. "I've gotten reacquainted with all the sailing hardware I can stand for one morning. Besides, in five minutes I might have an engagement, or maybe even an invitation to lunch." At one time Cade would have laughed and offered to share a sandwich. But not now. He didn't laugh and whatever he planned to eat for lunch he clearly did not mean to share with her.

The smallest hint of a smile tucked in the corner of his mouth, but it meant nothing. Autumn had seen that parody too often during the past several days to be fooled by it. "If you already have plans," he said, "then we'll talk when you return."

Her gaze fell to the pages in her hand. "I don't have plans. I only said that five minutes from now I *might* have plans. . . ." How ridiculous to explain

110

when he'd known what she meant. He'd simply chosen to ignore it. "Let's go."

She walked past him, chin in the air, heart beating rapidly. Cade fell into step behind her, not so close that she could feel the warmth of his breath on her hair, but close enough that she could imagine how it might feel.

Her imagination seemed to be at its irresponsible worst lately, conjuring up fantasies when she should have been thinking of other things. Things like confirming arrangements with workmen so the renovations could begin as soon as she heard from the bank. Things like why she was being summoned to his office and what he wanted to talk about. But she couldn't seem to concentrate on such things when he was anywhere near.

Cade stopped as they entered the reception area and Autumn paused inside his office doorway to look back. He was standing beside Marilynda's desk and the smile *she* received was genuine. "Hold my calls for a while, Marilynda," he said. "Autumn and I are having a . . . stockholders meeting."

Autumn dropped the inventory list she had been holding onto the desk and retreated to the window as Cade walked into the office and closed the door behind him. The room seemed to contract, the air vibrating with a tension that was too tangible to ignore, too sensitive to acknowledge. Clasping her hands in front of her, she watched him move to the desk. "The first official stockholders meeting in the history of Eastport, Inc.," she said teasingly. "I'm glad I was invited, but don't you think Ross should be here too?"

"I've just spoken with your brother on the telephone. He knows what you and I are going to discuss."

Autumn frowned her discouragement. Obviously Cade intended to take seriously every word she uttered. She turned to look at the parking lot outside the window, hoping to ease the tight pressure in her lungs. She heard the soft sound of leather yielding and knew that Cade had seated himself without waiting for her to do the same. Good. Maybe, at last, he was bending the rigid politeness of the past two weeks. She'd begun to think he was as stiff as the business suits he invariably wore to the office.

"Autumn, I've made a decision." A chill seeped through her with the note of determination in his voice. But as she pivoted toward him, a slow tide of awareness warmed her. He was watching her carefully, his blue eyes shadowed with an indefinable caution. A tug of sympathy pulled at her heart and she wondered if they would ever be completely at ease with each other again.

"A decision?" she asked. "What about?"

"Your boutique. Ross and I have decided you should go ahead with the idea. I phoned the bank this morning and was told it will be at least another week before they'll have an answer for you. James Clayton was called out of town and there doesn't seem to be anyone else authorized to make the credit approval."

Autumn couldn't help but smile. "You mean the bank's still open? I thought when the banker left town, he locked the bank doors behind him."

"Eastport isn't *that* small, Autumn." His gaze softened somewhat. "You've just been spoiled by the fast pace of the city. Things may move a little slower here, but they do move."

"I wasn't complaining, Cade."

"I know."

Their eyes held in a moment of understanding that was almost friendly, but wasn't quite natural. The tension altered suddenly, the cautious distance between them melting into a new and subtle closeness. Autumn looked away, afraid of what Cade might see, afraid of the futile wishes in her own heart.

"After I'd talked with the bank," he continued, ignoring—if he'd noticed at all—that brief moment of sharing, "I called Ross to ask his opinion about getting the work started right away."

She interrupted with a softly reticent laugh. "I'm sure my brother didn't hesitate to tell you either. He's already warned me not to come near the marina with any of my 'harebrained' ideas."

"No matter what he tells you, Autumn, he believes you can carry off this particular 'harebrained' idea on sheer tenacity."

"And do you believe that, Cade?" She faced him with an inquisitive and slightly challenging stare.

His lips formed a leisurely grin. "I happen to believe you're also going to need a hell of a lot of luck. But that's neither here nor there. I think the remodeling work should be done now. In another few weeks the weather will be too cold for the constant in-and-out flow of workmen and if we wait until spring, you'll get a late start on our busiest season."

"What about the line of credit? Shouldn't we wait to be sure the bank approves it?"

"I'll take care of that, Autumn. Don't worry about it."

A doubt wandered through her mind, slipped away, and returned. Two weeks before, Cade had been glad of an excuse to postpone a decision. Now he'd not only decided, he wanted to begin work right away. "Another week or so won't make that much difference," she said. "Then you can rest easy knowing I have something more substantial than tenacity with which to start the boutique."

"I thought this was what you wanted." Impatience lined his voice.

The doubt doubled in size and Autumn frowned. "Of course I'd love to open for business tomorrow, Cade, but I know that isn't realistic. I can wait until the bank—"

"I said I'd take care of that, Autumn. If Clayton turns you down, we'll get the line of credit somewhere else."

"But you said you'd prefer that the local—"

"Stop trying to look a gift-horse in . . ." He obviously thought better of finishing the sentence, but he didn't flinch from her sudden and equally obvious annoyance.

Doubt became certainty as her brown eyes clashed with his determined blue ones. She would have liked to vent her frustration with him in a tension-releasing anger, but some inner knowledge stayed her impulse. This unlooked-for capitulation was his way of appeasing her, of smoothing a strained situation. She knew it as well as she knew him. The new wariness in their relationship bothered him and he was seeking a way to please her, to make everything "right." And the ploy would have worked fifteen years ago, but she was no longer a child to be indulged. She opened her mouth to tell him so, and in the same instant knew it was not the sort of thing he could be told.

"Fine, Cade. I won't worry about the bank's decision." She couldn't control the cool edge of displeasure that laced her voice. "I'll get in touch with the construction people this afternoon, or have you already taken care of that for me?"

"No. This is your project, Autumn. I just wanted to—" He stroked a thumb along his jaw in ill-concealed irritation. "Hell, I thought you'd be happy about this."

"I *am* happy."

"Well, you could smile then."

"I don't *feel* like smiling!" She felt like telling him exactly what he could do with *his* plans for *her* project, but she forced her energy into picking up the inventory list she'd dropped on his desk. "I have too many things to do."

"You don't have to familiarize yourself with every last stock number in this store. I don't understand why you think that's so important all of a sudden."

It was a way of assuming a responsibility she'd left too long neglected, but Cade, of course, wouldn't credit her with such an adult motivation. Her grip on the papers firmed. "Maybe I'm just protecting my own interests, Cade. I haven't had much to do with the store's operation since I started college. Someday I might need to know exactly what my quarter of this business includes, and you might not be around to tell me."

"That's hardly likely."

"You never know." She lifted her shoulders in a shrug, but her throat ached with the effort to appear nonchalant. "At any rate, after today I'll have to concentrate on getting the boutique ready to open, now that I have your *permission* to begin. But don't think that I'll neglect the other aspects of this store. Not anymore."

He was on his feet, abandoning the position of authority to face her squarely. But as he rounded the corner of the desk, Autumn stepped back, clutching the inventory list like a shield. Cade stopped abruptly; whatever he'd been about to say to her was stilled by her defensive movement. She saw the question reflected in his sudden frown, but couldn't prevent her apprehension from weaving itself into the air between them. He was too close already. She was too aware. No matter what he thought, she couldn't let him come any nearer.

"I never intended to sound like I was granting permission, Autumn. I was only trying to—"

"I know what you're trying to do, Cade, and I know I'm supposed to be pleased. But I'm not. I'm just not and for heaven's sake, don't ask me to explain." She faltered when she saw the change in his expression, but then plunged on. "It would be pointless to argue about something we agree on. And I do agree with you that the sooner work gets under way the better. It's just that I wish you'd handled the situation with a little more . . . professionalism."

"Now, what in hell is that supposed to mean? This feels very much like an argument despite the fact that we're supposedly in complete agreement." He took a step forward and reached for the list in her hand.

Autumn retreated, taking the list with her. "I only meant that you'd made up your mind before you ever thought about asking my opinion. You asked Ross, but you simply told me what your decision was. I own as many shares of stock as my brother, yet he's treated as a partner while I'm treated like a—" She broke off. It was bad enough that he continued to think of her as a child; she didn't have to keep reminding him.

"Look, just forget it. You're happy. I'm happy. Let's leave it at that." She eyed the doorway behind him, wanting to escape, but not wanting to walk past him. "And speaking of leaving, I'm sure someone, somewhere, is waiting to take me to lunch, so if you don't mind . . ."

He didn't move. Autumn swallowed the knot of discomfort in her throat and started toward the door. As she reached his side, his fingers closed around her wrist and her heart took a swan dive to the bottom of her stomach. "Autumn?"

His husky voice calling her name relentlessly tugged her gaze up to meet his and her body trembled. For a moment she imagined giving in to the impulse to melt against him, to enclose him in her arms and in her love. Her hand crept to the base of her throat and hovered there uncertainly.

Doubt feathered the corners of his eyes and the grip on her wrist relaxed as he rubbed his thumb back and forth over her skin. The inventory list slipped from her fingers to slide aimlessly onto the floor. Her lips parted of their own volition to invite him, even though logic told her he had no intention of accepting. As if he were trying to interpret her silence, Cade bent slightly toward her and without conscious thought her hand went from her throat to pause a touch away from his cheek.

She hesitated, locked in that instant of decision, knowing she mustn't complicate an already complicated situation, but not knowing how to get her hand safely back to her side. Yet even as the thought took shape, Cade made the decision and stepped back, releasing her wrist and bending to retrieve the inventory list. When he straightened again, the ambiance of intimacy was gone, as if it had never been.

The curve of his mouth formed a familiar line of mischief that somehow failed to reach his eyes. "Get your things, Autumn, and I'll take you to lunch. All you have to do is smile."

She lowered her lashes to conceal the annoyance that returned in full measure with his words. "No, thank you." Gaining a modicum of control, she made herself face his pseudo-amusement. "My smiles don't come so cheaply anymore, Cade."

She was opening the office door in a matter of seconds and walking as casually as possible through the reception area. Cade's gaze was on her every step of the way and his silence thundered after her, but she kept walking. Ignoring Marilynda's concerned glance, Autumn left the office and entered the store itself. She paused just long enough to get

118

her jacket and purse before heading for the wide, wooden front door of Eastport Boat Supply.

"Wait, Autumn," Cade called behind her, but she didn't even glance back as she pulled on the door handle and stepped outside. At the curb a long, black limousine eased to a halt right behind the No Parking sign and Autumn had a sudden, panicky impulse to laugh aloud. All the tensions of the past two weeks coupled with the strain of the last few minutes culminated in the wild idea that she must be hallucinating. Richard Colburn had never, in all the time she'd known him, arrived anywhere on time. To think that he had arrived now, with such perfect split-second timing was funny. No, she amended as she heard the door of the boat supply open behind her. It wasn't funny, and if Richard's timing had been truly perfect, the limousine—with her inside—would at this very moment be sweeping away from the curb.

She felt Cade's displeasure, but knew if she turned to look, his expression would reveal only a mild curiosity. She didn't turn. She stepped forward to meet the tall slender man who was getting out of the car. Richard Colburn was darkly handsome, with beguiling eyes that occasionally were a somber sapphire, but usually sparkled a charming baby blue. His tailored suit matched the limousine in color and pampered elegance. A gold watch chain on his vest added a flavor of old-world, old-money dignity. Autumn knew, though, the watch in his pocket wouldn't have the correct time because Richard never bothered to set it.

"God! What a beautiful woman!" He met her in

the middle of the sidewalk, pulled her into his arms, and kissed her soundly. She was awkwardly conscious of Cade's presence and would have offered a more restrained greeting, but Richard didn't give her a chance to state her preference. When he drew back to hold her at arm's length, his lips curved disarmingly. "Hello. Could you tell me where in this thriving metropolis I might find a cherry pie?"

Autumn smiled a welcome. "Hello, Richard. What a surprise. How did you ever find your way down here?"

"I set the car on autopilot and here I am." He caught sight of Cade and turned expectantly. "I'm Richard Colburn," he said, extending his hand as he crossed the sidewalk.

"Kincade O'Connor." Cade reciprocated and shook the proffered hand with only a slight hesitation that Autumn was sure no one else would have noticed. Both men took a step back, smiled, and eyed the other warily.

"From all that Autumn's told me, I expected you to be taller," Richard said, innocently disregarding the fact that he had to look up to say it. "From the way she talked, I thought you'd be at least eight feet, but I suppose stature is in the eye of the beholder."

Cade glanced at Autumn, obviously unsure of how to reply. There was no need to answer, though, because Richard had turned his attention to the store window. "Great-looking display, Autumn."

The compliment pleased her all the more because Cade heard it. "Thank you," she said pointedly. "I've been taking care of the window since I returned. Cade doesn't really like to do it." Her smile deepened; Cade frowned.

"You're lucky to have her." Richard's gaze went from Autumn to Cade. "She's a natural when it comes to merchandising and I have every intention of stealing her away from you and taking her home to New York." He winked at her. "Are your bags packed?"

With a shake of her head, she tried not to notice Cade's frosty regard. "Would you like to see the store, Richard?"

"Do you have time to show me around, O'Connor?"

This time Cade smiled and Autumn frowned. "Of course," he answered as he opened the front door and motioned Richard inside. Autumn entered first, but soon found herself a step behind as the two men began talking business. She could have strangled Richard for assuming that Cade should be the tour guide. And as for Cade—well, he should have had the good grace not to notice.

For almost twenty minutes Autumn followed, listened, and responded with a polite nod whenever a comment was tossed in her direction. At last, though, Cade turned to her with the suggestion that she show Richard "her" corner of the store. She didn't quite understand how Cade managed to redeem himself in those few words, but she knew that her heart had quickened with the note of pride in his voice. He stood quietly at her side as she explained her plans for the mini-boutique. Richard was sincere in his praise, but it was Cade's silent approval that mattered, that brought the soft color to her cheeks.

"How soon will you be ready to open?" Richard asked.

"December first," Cade answered before Autumn had a chance.

Richard arched his brows in surprise. "Great. The sooner the better as far as I'm concerned. I'll be very glad when Autumn gets this small-town-success syndrome out of her system and comes home to New York, where she belongs."

The denial formed on her lips, a denial she'd made a hundred times and that Richard had predictably ignored each time, but it died when she heard Cade's brusque agreement. "So will I, Richard. So will I."

She could hardly believe he'd said it, but it was easy to believe he meant it. Through a hazy sense of betrayal, she heard Cade tell Richard what a pleasure it had been to meet him. She saw the polite handshake of farewell, and she saw Cade turn toward the office, but she refused to watch him go. Instead, she flashed Richard a warm smile and suggested a nice leisurely lunch.

"I know just the place." Richard took her hand and laced his fingers with hers. "It'll take a couple of hours to get there, but if you can take the afternoon off . . ."

"No problem." With a tip of her chin Autumn mentally consigned the inventory list and the entire boat supply business to the devil. "I own one-fourth of this store, so I don't have to ask permission."

"God, not only beautiful, but independent as well. Could I interest you in a trip to see my etchings?"

"At the moment I'm interested only in lunch."

"And after that?"

"I'm game for almost anything, as long as it's at least fifty miles from Eastport."

He grinned wickedly and his eyes twinkled a frivolous warning. "Lucky you. I just happen to know the perfect place." Richard made a grand sweep with his free hand toward the door and the chauffeured car waiting outside. "This way to paradise. . . ."

Autumn smiled at his nonsense and wished that Richard could whisk her magically away. She desperately needed to put some distance between herself and Cade. But in her heart she knew that Cade, not with her and uninvited, would be along for the entire trip—no matter how far away "paradise" proved to be.

CHAPTER SEVEN

Cade eyed the angle of the sun and decided that he had time to take the sailboat out for a few hours before dark. Not that he had to be in a hurry—the boat was equipped with lights and he knew the area like the back of his hand, but there was no reason to stay out on the bay that long. Once, late afternoon had been his favorite time of day for sailing, but that had been when he had Autumn for company, when her delight in watching the sunset from out on the water had made the extra effort of sailing home at night worthwhile.

He wondered how the sunset would look from the tinted windows of a limousine. Probably like a million dollars. With a grimace of distaste Cade stepped up onto the boat deck and took a deep, cleansing breath. He wished he could stop thinking about limousines and glitzy restaurants and the fact that Autumn hadn't come back to the store. She

124

hadn't been home either. He'd checked. Of course she'd only been gone since noon, but that was long enough.

Long enough. He rubbed the back of his neck and resolutely reminded himself that Autumn was not accountable to him. If she chose to take a lunch hour that lasted until next week, he had no right to protest. If he were honest, he would have to admit that he'd done little to encourage her to return.

Ever since the night he'd let things get out of control, he'd tried to discourage her from being anywhere near him. He'd ignored, as best he could, her presence at the store. He'd made no comment on the way she'd taken charge of the window display, and until today he'd said nothing about her quiet determination to relearn all of the things she'd forgotten about the boat supply business. Ross had even expressed his pleasant surprise at Autumn's newfound interest in the work done at the marina.

But Cade had remained silent despite the feeling of pride that would not be reasoned away, despite his longing to dispel the frown she so often wore. The distance he so carefully observed was a means of self-defense, of protecting himself as well as her.

But this morning he'd watched her methodically checking the inventory list and he'd known he had to do something to make her smile.

Cade began to release the snaps on the sail cover with unnecessarily sharp tugs. Richard Colburn had made her smile. And Richard Colburn had kissed her. And Richard Colburn had taken her to lunch . . . and hadn't brought her back.

The cover came loose and Cade began folding it. As far as he knew, Autumn might be in New York City at this very moment.

But she wasn't. He caught a glimpse of bright color on the path at the end of the dock and his heart jerked in recognition. Autumn had been wearing that particular shade of sunshine today. He hadn't been able to keep from noticing how the color had complemented her own vibrant loveliness. He'd often thought she was aptly named, but never more so than now as he watched her walking toward him.

Autumn. She was as vivid and breathtaking as the October world around her. And in that moment Cade knew how colorless the passing seasons had been without her. She was warmth in a winter snow; her husky voice was the laughter of spring; her eyes held the rich tawny heat of summer, and in autumn . . . she was magic.

She paused at the end of the path, her gaze meeting his in wary surprise. He thought that she might turn and leave, but after another few seconds of hesitation she walked onto the dock and stopped beside the boat. "Going out?"

He nodded, finished folding the sail cover, and moved to stow it in the bulkhead. Grabbing a couple of ring buoys from the storage space, he tossed them onto the cockpit bench and glanced at her. "Did you have a nice afternoon?"

She nodded, looked at the afternoon sky, looked back to him. "Would you like some company?"

It had taken a lot of effort to ask that question. Cade could see the subtle way she bit her lower lip;

he was no stranger to the wistful tilt of her chin and he had no immunity to the note of appeal in her voice. "Do you remember how to attach the jib?"

He was tempting fate, he knew, but her slow smile was worth the risk. She was on deck in a matter of moments, putting on the jacket she had been carrying, and then bringing her hand to her forehead in salute. "Of course, I remember," she said, her tone brimming with mischief. "Just point me in the right direction."

Solemnly he pointed back to the dock. Autumn laughed a throaty, lilting, seductive laugh, and Cade knew he was all kinds of a fool if he left the dock with her on board. But even as she set about proving that she did remember the correct procedure of fastening the jib, he defiantly began preparing to leave.

"Cast off the bow lines," he called as the motor purred to life. Autumn released the moorings and settled back as the boat glided forward. It had been a long time since she'd been sailing, and the anticipation made her pulse race. Her gaze slid to the helm where Cade stood, guiding their course slowly, carefully, away from the dock. Sailing had nothing to do with the rapid-fire beat of her heart, she admitted. It was Cade, his nearness, his tousled, sun-kissed hair, the sensuous blue of his eyes— Cade, who filled her with breathy tension.

He caught her look and returned it with a smile. "What happened to Richard?"

"He had to be in Washington tonight for some sort of reception."

"Didn't he invite you?"

As a matter of fact, Richard had invited her, had *implored* her in his usual unserious way. But Autumn merely shook her head in answer and focused her attention on the rhythmic dipping of the bow. She was glad to hear the note of friendly interest in Cade's voice, but she felt oddly disappointed that he could speak of Richard so casually.

Silence descended, a silence that was full of sounds but empty of meaning. What was Cade thinking? she wondered. Was he wishing that she had gone with Richard instead of inviting herself along for a sail? Was he wishing that Marilynda were here with him instead?

Oh, stop, she commanded herself. She had spent the entire afternoon thinking and wishing. Even Richard's ego-soothing, witty good humor hadn't made much of a dent in her low spirits. It was Cade's fault, wholly his responsibility. Or perhaps it was her own fault for growing up when Cade wasn't looking.

Autumn ran her fingers through her copper hair, waiting for the sailboat to clear the protected inlet, waiting for her restlessness to ebb, waiting for something she wasn't able to name. Her eyes sought Cade's and found him watching her. A quavery breath hung in her throat and sexual awareness caressed her with the zephyr softness of the breeze. Then, as if a sound of warning echoed like a siren's song, his gaze slid past her and she focused on the water breaking into ruffled waves with the boat's motion.

Let's sail around the moon, he'd suggested on some lighthearted yesterday and she, with nearsighted wisdom, had replied, *We can't get there from here.* Autumn sighed with the fleeting memory. How many opportunities to know him had she missed because her sights were set on distant dreams? And how many times had she listened without hearing all that his words revealed? More than she could possibly remember. And now she was caught in a tapestry of her own design, wanting more than friendship, but unable to unravel what she had so carefully woven. *We can't get there from here.* Maybe her careless answer had been more farsighted than she realized.

The boat swayed as it caught the breeze and Autumn scrambled to her feet to help Cade hoist the mainsail. Once under way, she refused to think past the moment, past the crisp whisper of the sails, and the feel of the wind and the sea spray. Within minutes it was like dozens of other times she'd been with Cade on the boat—the enjoyment of sailing bringing a common bond, a familiar comradeship to their thoughts.

Time raced with the wind and Autumn was unaware of its passage until Cade pointed toward the west. "Do you want to watch the sunset?" he asked, and she followed his gaze to the rosy aura that rimmed the sky.

"Could we?" It had been such a long time since she'd seen the day end from this perspective, too long since she'd taken time to enjoy the natural wonders around her.

In answer, Cade guided the craft closer to the wind-protected shore, and Autumn helped him anchor it. She sank onto the foredeck, hugging her knees and preparing to lose herself in a magnificent Chesapeake sunset. Feeling Cade watching her, she turned toward him with an inviting smile. "The show's about to begin. Would you like to share my front-row seat?"

"No."

He was so still, so unnaturally still, that her smile faded as the restless wind stirred inside her. His eyes held hers with a curious restraint, and she couldn't have looked away if she'd tried.

Abruptly he swung toward the cabin door. "I'm going to get something to drink." His words reached her as he disappeared from sight into the cabin.

Autumn sat for a full minute, listening to his movements belowdecks, wondering why it was suddenly so difficult to breathe. Maybe she, too, needed a drink. Maybe, more than that, she needed to talk to Cade, to finally, once and for all, heal the rift in their relationship. She was on her feet then, her mind searching for the right words, as she stepped down into the narrow confines of the cabin.

"Cade?" Her eyes had to adjust to the interior light, but still she saw him tense with the sound of her voice. Hadn't he heard her footsteps? No, she knew somehow that he hadn't, that he hadn't expected her to follow and that he had been deep in thought. "Cade," she whispered softly, hesitantly, "could I talk to you for a . . ." The question died when he faced her fully, his eyes shadowed, but intense, as they met hers.

"Talk?" He repeated before taking a long swallow from the can of soda he held. Then he placed the can on the counter loudly. The seconds stretched into an eternity of deafening silence that seemed to grow with every heartbeat.

"Autumn, unless you get out of this cabin right now, something is going to happen that will spoil a very long and beautiful friendship."

She absorbed his words slowly, never looking away from the blue eyes that warned her to run from him. But she couldn't. She was helpless, caught between the knowledge that he was going to make love to her and her own aching desire to know him in that new and intimate way. Once it happened, there could be no going back and yet, Autumn knew that she had passed the point of no return long before this moment of decision. With love—and fear—in her heart, she stepped toward him.

Cade closed his eyes as she took that first tentative step and he tried to reason with the desire that burned hot and uncontrollable inside him. He reminded himself of the multitude of good solid reasons why he should not allow the inevitable to happen, but it *was* inevitable. He couldn't stop it. There wasn't an argument strong enough to counteract the gentle brush of her arms as they went around his neck and he didn't have the strength of will to resist the invitation of her lips. *Heroes be damned!* he thought as he lifted her against him. He was, after all, only a man.

He claimed her mouth with a passion too long denied, and wondered at the eagerness of her response. Her hands cupped at his nape and pressed him down into the warmth of her kiss. Like a sun-drop opening to the dawn, her lips parted beneath his, her tongue seeking and finding his. Hot spirals of need raced through him and he crushed her even closer as his thoughts swirled into one consummate desire.

His hands ran the length of her body, stopping at the slender curve of her hips. He stroked her, searching for the fastening of her clothing that kept him from touching her skin. A soft, aching moan vibrated against him and split the driving purpose of his consciousness. Slowly, carefully, he eased away from her and took a moment to look at her. Eyes closed, dark lashes feathered on cheeks tinted with longing, red-gold hair framing her creamy features with fire. At last she was in his embrace. After so many empty dreams she was holding him, returning his kisses, wanting him as he had wanted her for so very long.

But that was no excuse for the fierce, throbbing, mindless passion that possessed him. He loved this woman more than he had ever loved anyone or anything. Whether this was illusion or reality, he didn't care to know. He knew only that this first time with her must be as gentle and tender as a love song.

Drawn by the faint trembling of her lips, he caressed the corner of her mouth, tasting, sipping, delighting, in the feel of her. "Autumn," he murmured huskily against the smoothness of her cheek.

"Yes, Cade," she whispered in her own throaty tones, knowing that he wasn't asking and she wasn't answering. The sound of their names blending into the air was simply a recognition, an acknowledgment of this perfect moment. Autumn wondered how she could have spent so much of her life searching for just such a moment without ever once realizing that it could be found in his arms.

Her palms moved to the lean angle of his jaw and conformed to the roughly textured shape. Cade. She knew, to the last crease tucked into his smile, how he looked. She had studied every line, every expression of his face, but she had never known the feel of him until now.

His fingers massaged the top of her thigh. She sighed and swayed closer to him, letting the delicious sensations drift over her. When his lips moved lightly to the sensitive hollow below her ear, she turned to invite his exploration down to the slope of her shoulder. Pushing the collar of her jacket aside, Cade traced a path of slow wonder to the base of her throat. Then he grasped the zipper pull of the jacket and tugged it leisurely downward.

His hand slipped inside to close over her breast and begin a more devastating caress. The jacket slipped from her shoulders to bind her arms and Autumn tried to shrug free, but with every movement she was held tighter. As Cade became aware of her struggle he took advantage of the situation by parting her blouse and nudging aside the lacy edge of her bra. His mouth drew pleasure to the rosy peak of her breast and the ache in her stomach danced lower.

Autumn murmured a sound of protest and knew that she had never felt so incomplete, so empty. When he lifted his head and began releasing her from the jacket's restraint, she could only gaze at him through a mist of need. With his assistance she slipped out of the jacket and unbuttoned her blouse. As if he couldn't bear to hurry even a single moment of the sweet anticipation, Cade removed her blouse one inch at a time. His gaze touched the satiny bareness of her skin and fanned the embers already burning inside her.

Once begun, there seemed no reason to increase the deliberate legato rhythm that guided her hands as she unfastened the waist of her pants so that he could remove them too. He bent to pull them to the floor, but stopped to slide the shoes she wore from her feet before stripping the slacks away. Then she stood, trembling with a dozen uncertainties as he slid her silken underwear unhurriedly down her legs. His hand cupped her calf and made a smooth sweep upward.

She halted his progress then, her fingers moving to satisfy her own half-formed plans. His coat was easily discarded, but his shirt was a pullover style, and after an awkward try, Cade gripped the hem and jerked it up and off. Autumn stared with veiled desire at the hair on his chest, realizing after a few hungry seconds that she could touch him, kiss the bronzed skin, run her fingers through that tantalizing male texture. And she did, hesitantly at first, but becoming bolder as she recognized his enjoyment.

When the rest of his clothing lay carelessly on the floor, she let her gaze discover him in the same way he was discovering her. She reveled with the ability to investigate at will, to linger whenever and wherever she wanted. And she granted him the same privilege, although she knew it was not within her power to deny him. When his hand rubbed the length of her body from shoulder to thigh, Autumn remembered the restraining barrier she still wore. Suddenly she was self-consciously aware of her nakedness and she turned from his gaze to remove her bra with belated discretion.

There was a low, tender sound of amusement before he grasped her shoulders and tugged her against him. Then his lips were warm in her hair and moving over her bare back. He trailed a row of tiny, nibbling kisses across her shoulders and down to the indentation of her waist before winding his way again to the hollows of her throat. Finally, when she thought she surely would fall into the weightless, floating sensations around her, he turned her in his arms, lifted her, and carried her the few steps to the bed.

He held her, supporting her weight as easily as he always had supported her hopes and dreams. With fingers clasped at his neck, Autumn saw the uncertainty in his eyes and matched it with understanding. The hesitation she felt in him and in her heart was merely a pause, an interlude in their blending, like the cadence of a song that built to crashing chords, softened, and then flowed back with a new intensity.

She breathed his name and his lips came slowly to whisper a promise to hers. In his kiss she savored the familiar and the new; she absorbed the quiet sharing of a moment that never had been before and never could be again. From her earliest memories she had loved him, but not like this, never like this. And once the intimate knowledge of him became hers, she never again could love him in quite the same way she loved him at this moment. The past had built the chords of this special love song, the future would flow with a new and intense melody, but for now she held the song in her heart and an elusive butterfly fluttered within her hands.

When he gently placed her on the bed, Autumn smiled and relinquished her claim to his lips. She waited with infinite patience for him to settle next to her before she gave in to the desire that spiraled through her. He drew her close against him, molding her to his form and creating a wealth of needs inside her. His fingers stroked her skin until she was breathy and hot and lost to all but his touch.

When at last he turned her beneath him, she sank down into waves of ecstasy, pulling Cade with her until she was completely covered with his sinewy heat. She wrapped herself around him, enfolded him in her love, and let his kiss consume her. Winds of passion blew balmy and seductive as her movements became a rhythmic harmony with his. And then, for one eternal instant, Autumn knew conquest and surrender, giving and receiving, the exquisite union of heart and body, and the separateness of two lives flowing into one. For that moment she knew what loving really meant.

For a long time afterward she lay in the curve of his arm, analyzing the wondrous sensations settling within her. Never before had she known the contentment, the total "rightness" of belonging as she now belonged to Cade. It was beautiful, beyond any emotion she'd ever experienced, and it was frightening. Her heart, her body, even her thoughts, could never be completely hers again. Never. In loving him she had given a part of herself that couldn't be reclaimed. Did he know? Over the years he had understood so many things that she was unable to express. Did he understand now how very much she loved him and how much his tender, physical expression of love had meant to her?

She must tell him, put the feelings into a spoken pledge. She needed to know that he understood. But how could she say, "Cade, I love you"? She had misused those words so often and yet she had always said them sincerely. How could she say them now when they could so easily be misinterpreted, when they might sound insincere or motivated simply by the physical contentment of the moment?

One of his hands rested lightly on her waist and she gently threaded her fingers with his. He had been special to her since the first moment of meeting, but never more so than now. Now she knew the deeper meaning of loving and giving; now he was both friend and lover; now, at last, she was home.

"Cade, I love you." As she said the words they were barely more than a whisper and the sentence hovered uncertainly between them. Autumn would have liked to pull the words from the air and embroider them with sincerity, but she didn't know how. It was very different, and infinitely harder to say "I love you" when her whole being ached with the meaning of those special words.

She held her breath and waited for his response, but as one silent second after another slipped by, her heartbeat escalated in apprehension. What was he thinking? What was he feeling? Why didn't he say something? *Anything?*

Fear, insidious and uninvited, wound its way into her thoughts. He couldn't have made love to her if he didn't love her, could he? Not Cade. Not with her. And yet . . . There was the doubt, the fear, developing in her logic. Other men, ordinary men, might make love without emotion, without commitment. But not Cade. Never Cade.

He shifted to the edge of the berth and swung his feet to the floor. She watched the tight play of muscles across his back, sensed his tension and told herself that at any moment he would turn and smile and say, "I love you." Even when he stood and began to dress, keeping his back to her all the time, she kept reassuring her heart. *He loves me. Of course he loves . . .*

But when he left the cabin without a word or a glance, she knew he didn't. She had seen his feelings as she wanted to see them. Against his warnings, she had backed friendship into a corner and had forfeited any chance of ever mending their once close relationship. Overhead, she could hear his movements and knew he was preparing to weigh anchor. He was taking her home—as if she were a child who had broken the rules.

With that thought Autumn rolled from the mattress and dressed quickly. She ran unsteady fingers through her hair and glanced at the doorway. No matter how risky or uncomfortable, she had to talk to him. Somehow, she must make him understand, she told herself as she went to find him.

The sunset was a streak of memory in the sky, but

138

she gave it only a cursory glance, searching instead for the blue of Cade's eyes. Even when she called his name, he didn't acknowledge her presence, not by a word or by a look. He just kept moving, stowing the anchor and anchor lines, adjusting the jib sheets, guiding the sailboat into open water, purposely ignoring her presence.

"Cade, I want—I have to—" Her stammered plea gained his attention, but brought no satisfaction. He simply stared hard at her, effectively killing whatever she had wanted to say.

"Don't, Autumn."

"But, Cade, I— We just—"

"No! It shouldn't have happened. I shouldn't have! Just leave it before I regret—" Cade bit back the word and closed his heart to the stricken expression on her face. Dear God! What was he saying? He already had a thousand regrets and he felt sure they would stay with him for the rest of his life.

For a few foolish moments he'd let himself believe that Autumn came to him freely, released from past expectations and emotions. He'd even imagined that they had reached a turning point, that there would be a real basis for building a new and different relationship. And he had wanted to believe it, had wanted to believe that she would be in his arms every night from now until forever.

I love you. Her husky voice echoed within him and his hand trembled as he gripped the helm. Why had he felt he must put an immediate and imperative distance between them? Why couldn't he take her quiet confession at face value? Why had his illusions crumbled with her words? Because she had said them so many times before.

Oh, Cade, I love you, she had told him on her eleventh birthday when he'd given her a necklace with a tiny genuine diamond. *I love you,* she had offered as comfort on the day of his father's funeral. *I love you, Cade,* she had said at fifteen when he'd spent hours patching her first broken heart. *Don't forget—I love you,* had been her parting words almost six years ago as she'd boarded a plane for new worlds and new horizons.

If only she hadn't said it now. If only she hadn't reminded him that "I love you" could mean many different things. And it could be said to many different people.

Cade stared in concentrated study at the twilight deepening in the water and fought the persistent doubts. But he couldn't stop himself from wondering how often Autumn had pledged her love, and to whom. Richard Colburn? Undoubtedly she had said those words to Richard. When? In the backseat of a limousine? In a fancy restaurant? In other, more intimate surroundings?

God! He drew in a long breath of self-disgust. Had he expected her to be inexperienced? Had he thought that she would come back to him as the same trusting, innocent child she'd been when she left? No, he hadn't expected her to come back at all. But she had. She had come home with experiences and disillusionments he knew nothing of and had had no part in shaping. He wasn't sure he knew any of the important things about her anymore. And he

140

wasn't at all sure what she'd meant when she'd said I love you.

But she had touched him, kissed him, caressed him. She had responded to his lovemaking as if there never before had been, or ever could be again, any other love for her. So why did the doubts continue to grow stronger? Why did he feel that there had been no depth of commitment on her part?

It was entirely possible that she had come to him because she needed comfort and reassurance. Autumn had sought the shelter of his arms more than once in the past when she needed someone—anyone. Was that the answer? Richard Colburn had driven back into her life today . . . and left without her. Had she been disappointed that Richard hadn't taken her with him? Was she planning to return to New York at some indefinite point in the future?

Cade scanned the darkness beyond the boat's lights, looking for familiar landmarks and wishing the dock were in sight. He wanted to be home, where he could put a reasonable distance between himself and Autumn. There would be no escape from the questions, he knew that. And there would be no easy answers either. But he needed time to think, to analyze what had happened and what kind of relationship, if any, he and Autumn could build now.

Without intending to, he turned to look at her and wished immediately that he hadn't. She sat sideways on the cockpit bench, very near to him, and yet she might have been miles away. Her arms encircled her bent legs and her forehead rested wearily on her knees. The moonlight dusted her hair with gold and his throat closed over the intense longing to touch her again. *Autumn, oh, Autumn.*

When the boat reached the dock, Autumn lifted her head and automatically rose to help with the mooring lines. Cade said nothing and she didn't linger in the stifling atmosphere. Her heart suggested a dozen things she might have said, but Autumn knew it was pointless even to say good night. He wouldn't hear, wouldn't listen. She had told him she loved him and he had answered with silence. She might not understand the distance he had placed between them, but she knew it could not be bridged from her side.

We can't get there from here. Her own words, light and laughing in memory, weighted her steps with loneliness as she walked up the path alone.

CHAPTER EIGHT

Autumn slept little that night. She stood at her bedroom window, alternately holding the curtain open and pulling it closed. The bed provided a place to lie when she grew tired of standing; the pillow offered a cushion for thoughts too heavy to hold upright; the scene below her window gave her something to stare at while the never-ending questions rolled wearily through her mind. *It shouldn't have happened,* he had said. But it had.

From window to bed to window, she paced, occasionally dozing fretfully in between. Morning came with a headache and a phone call.

"Autumn? This is Cade." He sounded as if he were a world away. Her heart plummeted to her feet, then soared to quiver in her throat. Everything she would have liked to say became tangled in memories of how very close they had been only hours before. "Autumn?" he repeated, so calmly, so coolly.

She could hardly believe it was his voice and she could hardly believe she stood, stupidly silent, gripping the phone as if her existence would shatter if she dropped it. "Yes?" At last she managed a solid, if somewhat shaky, answer.

"I know it's early, but—" His easy confidence seemed to desert him at that point and he said nothing for the space of several heartbeats. "Autumn, are you all right?"

No. She was never going to be all right again. But the tenderness, the familiar attempt to comfort that edged his voice, prevented her from saying so. "Yes," she lied. Her voice had an underlying crispness to it, an almost brittle tone.

Silence trembled along the phone lines and surrendered to caution. "I'm leaving for Annapolis this morning," he said, "and I won't return until after the sailboat show. Can you handle things at the store? It'll be next weekend before I—"

"That's fine. Everything will be fine," she hastened to interrupt, to stop the bittersweet ache she felt at being suddenly separated from him, but she hadn't intended to sound indifferent. In the past that had been a sure signal to Cade. He'd never failed to pick up on the hurt that hid behind her show of unconcern.

At least, he'd never *before* failed to notice. "Then I won't worry. I know how much you love to take charge."

God! She could have killed him for using that teasing tone. Now, of all times. How could he? But still he went on. "I'll expect to see swimsuits in the window when I get back."

"Don't set your expectations too high."

His pause was a mere breath of quiescence. "No. I won't do that. If you need any help—"

She replaced the receiver with a click and Cade felt his grip on the telephone go slack. He stared at the instrument in his hand before he returned it to the cradle. It made a hollow, synthetic clatter and he frowned. Only a moment ago he'd heard the rich huskiness inherent in Autumn's voice and yet there had been a new inflection. She might have been sleepy—had she been able to sleep? Had she dreamed of him? No, he would have recognized the sound of drowsiness. It was something different, something he'd never heard before, at least not from Autumn. Caution perhaps? Disappointment? Regret?

It didn't matter. Later he would wonder how she felt, what she thought, but not now. Not when he was close enough to follow that phone call with a visit. Not when he was in a mood to ask questions that he had no right to ask. Not when he would demand answers that he wasn't sure he wanted to hear.

No. He'd been unprepared for her to return, unprepared for the changes in her and totally, completely, unprepared for the inevitability of what had happened between them last night. *Say it*, his mind commanded, but he shunned the thought and walked to the window. There across the yard, beyond the hedge, just above the spiky top of the evergreen tree, was Autumn's window. Was she there now, watching him, thinking of him as he was her?

Admit it, came the whisper of conscience again. Cade closed his eyes and remembered the feel of her in his arms, the taste and sight and scent of her as they'd made love. Slowly he opened his eyes and absorbed the meaning of the words. Last night he had made love to Autumn. No, his lips curved gently in correction. Last night he had made love *with* Autumn. For the first time in his life he understood the difference.

He hadn't allowed himself to say it or even think it until now. The tender reality of loving her and the chafing irritation of doubting her weren't compatible. And so he hadn't let his thoughts dwell on either one. He'd lain on the bed, staring at the ceiling and planning—careful, complicated planning that brought no resolution or comfort. He would go to Annapolis immediately. The boat show was only a few days away and offered a logical excuse for putting Autumn safely out of his reach. There were people he needed to see at the boat show, things he could do, but above all he would be able to think, to decide how to cope with the change in his relationship with her. When he saw her again, he would be prepared.

Purposefully he turned from the window and surveyed the room. The bed with all the wrinkles smoothed from sight, the suitcase that was packed and waiting, the now silent telephone that could convey so much or so little. He shouldn't have phoned her, but he couldn't just leave without a word. That was too much like running away, and he wasn't running. He simply had to have some time.

Cade crossed the room and lifted the suitcase, knowing he must go, wanting instead to go to Autumn, to talk to her, share with her. . . .

But that was what he had to discover. It might never again be possible to be with Autumn, to really talk with her, to share with her . . . to make love with her.

He had to face his doubts, his limitations, and his alternatives. He must decide what he could dare to hope for and what he might have to settle for. *Don't set your expectations too high,* he warned himself.

With a heavy and heartfelt sigh he walked from the room and closed the door behind him.

Autumn slumped into the easy comfort of Cade's office chair and propped her feet on the corner of his desk. Beyond the closed door of the office, saws whined and hammers banged. She hadn't realized it would take quite so much noise to redo one relatively small corner of the store. Enthusiasm among the employees had waned noticeably since the work commenced, and Autumn was becoming adept at smiling and nodding sympathetically when customers complained.

Small wonder that Ross had made only a brief appearance to "check on the progress" before he and Lorna left for Annapolis. They had gone just for the weekend, returning on Sunday with an evening's worth of "You should have been there," and "You'll never guess who we ran into," and other interesting details about the sailboat show. Autumn had been interested, but she'd really wanted to ask if they'd seen Cade and what he was doing and if he'd, by any chance, asked about her. His name had drifted into the conversation only once, though, and then Lorna had merely commented that he'd seemed preoccupied.

With a frown Autumn picked up a rubber band from the desktop and idly wrapped it around her finger. Obviously he must still be preoccupied, as it was now Wednesday and he hadn't returned or even phoned. She had thought he would at least check on how things were going at the store, but if he did, the calls stopped short of reaching her.

Marilynda had probably set his mind at rest over the weekend. She, too, had attended the boat show and returned to the office with glowing accounts of all she'd learned. But there'd been no mention of Cade, except in an offhand, impersonal way.

Autumn couldn't keep from wondering how a weekend with Cade could be impersonal, but then, her perspective wasn't exactly unbiased at the moment. With a grimace of distaste for her train of thought, she flipped the rubber band across the room and turned her attention to the letter lying open on her lap. The message hadn't changed. It still conveyed a firm, uncompromising *no*. The bank had denied her request for a line of credit.

James Clayton had phoned the day before to warn her that the letter was coming and to explain why he'd had to refuse. She'd listened, although she really didn't want to hear that the bank was being more conservative in these uncertain economic times; that at this time the bank couldn't afford to extend credit to a new and somewhat uncertain business venture; that the bank regretted its inability to help a valued customer, but if the bank could be of any service at a later date . . . The explanations had rolled on in the same abstract vein until Autumn had finally concluded the conversation with an insincere thank you and a meaningful goodbye.

Cade had said if the Eastport bank turned down her request, he would help her get the credit elsewhere. She began folding the corners of the letter as she decided that, at least, the subject of money would be an effective icebreaker when he returned. If that didn't restore a measure of equanimity between them, nothing could.

His reaction to the bank's denial of credit and to the remodeling work already done would tell her a lot about how he planned to treat the undeniable fact that they had passed the point of friendship. A slow, sweet shiver ebbed through her as it did every time she thought of making love with him. Would she ever stop remembering? Would she be able to act as if it had never happened?

No, and she wasn't even going to try. She and Cade were going to talk, regardless of how he might feel about it. Just as soon as he came home . . . The letter, folded into a neat airplane, sailed across the room on the wings of her resolve and landed on the edge of the windowsill. It dipped indecisively toward the floor, righted itself, then dipped again. Autumn reached for another rubber band and placed it carefully on her fingertip.

"Glad to see you're keeping busy." Cade's voice

came from the doorway and made her drop her feet from the top of his desk with a guilty start. The rubber band fell to the floor in unison with the paper plane and she swiveled the chair around to face him.

Leaning against the doorjamb, dressed in deck shoes, weathered jeans, and a soft plaid flannel shirt partially hidden by the navy Windbreaker he wore, Cade looked so endearingly familiar that Autumn couldn't contain her smile. It widened in greeting and with the sheer pleasure of seeing him again.

She took another rubber band from the drawer and twirled it artfully around her finger. "It's a dirty job," she said with a saucy little shrug, "but someone's got to do it."

His lips slanted a slow response and his eyes warmed to a summer-sky blue. "I've been telling you that for years, but you've always insisted *I* should do it."

"I haven't changed my mind, Cade. After all, fair is fair and you do own twice as much of this place as I do."

"Does that mean you're ready to relinquish the seat of authority?"

She relaxed against the chair back. "The job, yes. The chair? No way. I'm claiming one-fourth of this office and at the moment that includes a place to sit."

"And all the rubber bands in my desk drawer," he said as he moved away from the doorway—leaving the door noticeably open—to sit in one of the chairs across from her. "Remodeling is hard work, isn't it?"

"Did you see what's been done?" Enthusiasm, kept too long to herself, bubbled to the surface and she forgot everything else except sharing it with Cade. "I had no idea the work would go so fast. They're going to finish by Saturday and then I have to arrange for the staining, painting, and carpeting to be done—wait until you see the carpet I chose. I can hardly believe it, Cade, there is actually going to be one corner of the store that has honest to goodness carpeting."

"Yes. I can hardly believe that myself." A wry smile punctuated the droll comment. "I looked around before I came into the office. It's really taking shape, Autumn. Another week and you'll be stocking bathing suits on the shelves and vacuuming the carpet every five minutes."

"A little more than a week, Cade. Things don't move quite that fast, even in New York. I'm going to have to make a couple of buying trips before we can begin to think about stocking the shelves."

"You're going to New York?" The question was brusque and quick.

Autumn hesitated, suddenly aware of her tension, suddenly aware that she wanted to kiss him. "Yes," she said, and wondered how he could miss the significance of her deeply indrawn breath. "Next week. And after that I'm going to Dallas to look for merchandise. It's going to take some speedy footwork to get the boutique stocked and ready for business in just a few weeks. I'll probably have to settle for a limited inventory to begin with, but next year . . ."

"How long are you staying?"

With a blink of confusion she sorted through his change of subject. "In Dallas? Four days."

"No, how long are you staying in New York?" He appeared relaxed and at ease, but Autumn sensed that the illusion cost him considerable effort.

"Only as long as it takes to get what I want."

His eyes narrowed, then turned to the window. "We're going to have to talk, Autumn."

She inhaled sharply and her heart pounded furiously against her ribs. Odd, how confidence and courage could vanish without a trace when confronted with vulnerable reality. "Oh? What about?" God, why did she sound so blasé?

The room filled suddenly with an unseen, but pulsating presence, a tight, nerve-shattering quiet that was as real as it was intangible. Cade kept his gaze on the window; his fingers curved over the arm of the chair. Slowly he lowered his gaze to the floor and stopped. His expression creased in puzzlement before he moved to get the letter airplane. As he unfolded the page, he straightened and then read in silence.

Autumn willed her pulse to take advantage of the respite and prepare for a personal, and emotionally risky, discussion. When he turned to her, though, there was no hint of any deep emotion in his eyes.

"Weren't you going to tell me about this?"

"Of course, but I didn't want to hit you with it the moment you walked through the door."

"Why not? You've never hesitated to present me with your problems before."

A frown tugged persistently at her mouth. "I wasn't hesitating. It just didn't seem so important that I had to blurt it out the minute I saw you. You'd already told me we'd get the line of credit somewhere else if the Eastport bank turned us down."

"Us?" He read the letter again. "This is your project, Autumn. Don't forget that, but I'll talk to James and see what I can find out about this."

"I've already talked with him—at length."

"And he won't reconsider?"

She shook her head. "Not unless I can magically produce more collateral. My interest in the company, for instance."

"I don't want you to do that," he stated unequivocally.

"I may not have any other choice."

His gaze slid to her and lingered for a thoughtful instant. "Are you positive you really want to do this, Autumn?"

"The boutique? Yes, Cade, I'm positive."

A gentle smile tipped his lips. "All right then. Don't worry, Autumn. I'll take care of this for you."

It wasn't the words as much as their indulgent tone that stripped away the years and made her feel like an awkward adolescent eagerly discarding problems and responsibilities on Cade's capable shoulders. She shattered the image in a slow, purposeful voice. "I'd prefer you didn't."

His expression became guarded then, questioning and faintly cautious. "Why not?"

"As you said, this is my project. And that includes handling the problems. I *can* handle this, you know."

"It could be more difficult than you expect."

"Don't worry, Cade. I'll get the line of credit."

"While you're in New York?"

"I don't know. That's a possibility, I suppose."

He dropped the bank's letter onto the edge of the desk and shoved a hand into his jacket pocket. "Then you don't need my help."

Autumn sighed, wondering how the first easy moments of sharing had led to this defensive exchange. "Cade, I—Of course, I need your help. I would never have considered opening the boutique if I hadn't known I could depend on you. But there are just some things I have to do myself. I can't let you take care of every problem for the rest of my life."

"In that case, I respectfully withdraw my offer of assistance and suggest that you allow me to take charge of *my* section of this office." He spoke lightly, but she saw the heaviness in his eyes and felt the cool distance return to taunt her.

She stood because it seemed to be what he expected her to do, but when he walked around the desk she made no move to step aside. Her heart made a soft murmur of protest when he ignored her nearness and slipped off his jacket and hung it on the back of the chair. In a moment he would have to turn to her, would have to touch her, and in that split-second Autumn ached with the need to say, *I love you, Cade. I want you to take care of my problems for the rest of my life.*

He turned then, but he didn't look directly at her. His attention was focused on the desktop clutter, and as his hands touched her waist to move her out of his way, she knew she didn't have the courage to voice her need aloud.

He seated himself and leafed through a few ma-

154

rina orders before his gaze shifted to hers. "Thanks for watching the office while I was gone, Autumn. Any problems? I mean any that you couldn't handle?"

"No." *None, except for being desperately in love with you and desperately afraid to tell you so.*

"Good." He lifted the stack of mail and began sorting through it.

Autumn swallowed, took a deep breath, and released it. "I—was there something you wanted to talk about?"

He tensed, and for the first time, looked uncomfortable. "I don't think this is the right time, Autumn. Maybe when you get back from New York . . . if you decide to come back."

"If I decide?" Her eyes flashed in sudden amazement and anger. "Is that what you think, Cade? That once I get to New York again I'll just forget about coming back to Eastport? Do you believe I'd simply change my mind about the boutique without a second's consideration for the time and money already invested?"

To his credit, he didn't say it aloud, but Autumn heard it in his challenging silence, knew the thought he hid from her view. *It wouldn't be the first time.* And she suddenly realized that to him the boutique was nothing more than dozens of other projects she'd undertaken in the past. A way to channel her energy and soothe her restless spirit, a new goal to pursue until a brighter star caught her eye.

Cade doubted her. The truth seeped through her

155

mind and clogged in her throat. She turned from him quickly, making her way to the doorway.

"Autumn!" he called, and she stopped as she heard the sound of his footsteps behind her. "Autumn, I . . ."

The stillness inside her was edged with hope, but woven with dread. Cade didn't believe in her ability to act responsibly or to carry a plan through to completion. She would have to prove herself to him, even though it seemed unfair and unnecessary. If there were anyone in the world who should know her, who should understand and accept her, it was Cade. But if he needed proof, she would give it. Maybe in some intangible way it would show him how much she loved him, not because she needed his help, but because she needed him.

If only he would touch her now, just place his hand on her shoulder or accidentally brush his fingers against her hair. . . .

The phone buzzed a demanding intrusion and he retraced his steps to the desk. "Yes?" he answered as he watched Autumn walk from the room and through the reception area. He'd hurt her and he hadn't meant to do that. As he settled back into the chair, he stared at the ceiling, his immediate attention on the telephone conversation, but his thoughts with Autumn.

As he replaced the receiver in its cradle he rubbed his temples and decided he was a first-rate coward. He had spent countless hours during the past week thinking, debating, questioning, and reaching a decision, only to have his courage desert him at the first glimpse of Autumn. She had seemed genuinely glad to see him and for a few minutes he'd thought everything might be all right, but when it came to voicing the emotion he felt so deeply, he'd hesitated, and the opportunity had vanished.

He'd come home intending to be honest. He had planned to tell her that he loved her, that he knew she would need time to adjust to the idea, but that he was willing to wait. And he'd been prepared—or so he'd thought—to accept whatever decision she made. But he'd seen her eager smile of greeting and he'd known he couldn't accept just any decision she gave him. It was all or nothing. And in those first moments his plans had seemed too risky, so he'd looked for an excuse to delay—and found one.

He didn't understand how the bank could have turned her down and yet, hadn't he half hoped that they would? Then she would have to turn to him; she would need his help and in some inexplicable way she would understand that he needed her. But she had made it crystal-clear that she could manage on her own. She was intent on proving him wrong, on showing him how independent and grown-up she could be, and though he didn't intend to, he seemed to spur that stubborn determination every time she was within ten feet of him.

He stopped massaging his temples, but the dull pounding inside went on and, with a rueful frown, he realized Autumn's boutique was already supplying him with a good-sized headache. The busy sounds vibrating through the building reminded him that it was too late to wish that Autumn would forget the whole idea. She was committed and he knew he'd been unfair when he'd made the comment about her staying in New York. She would be back; if only because he'd voiced a doubt that she would.

And in the meantime he could only hope his courage would develop a stronger resolve. Maybe when she returned from the buying trips, he would be able to tell her what he'd wanted to tell her today. Who would ever have thought it could be so difficult to say *I love you* to the woman he'd loved with all his heart for so many years?

CHAPTER NINE

It was quiet inside the store. The Sunday-quiet was disturbed only by the occasional bristly sound of thunder. No customers. No salespeople. No muffled drone of busyness. Just a nice soft quiet that wrapped Autumn in contemplation as she worked.

The display case shone a crystalline clean, but she pointed the spray bottle at the glass top and misted the surface one more time. As she polished, Autumn mentally inventoried the contents of the case again and wondered if she should switch the sun visors from the lower shelf to the upper. No, she had done so twice already and decided both times she should have left well enough alone.

She had arranged and rearranged every single item, had dusted and polished every square inch and still she could hardly believe that the boutique was ready for next week's grand opening. It had taken many long, exhausting hours, three trips to

New York, one trip to Dallas, and several sleepless nights, but at last her idea had come to life.

The carpet smelled new, felt cushiony, and lent a touch of cheery color to the renovated corner. Shelves lined the walls, circular suspension racks held neatly aligned hangers that in turn held blouses, jackets, shirts, shorts, slacks, and various other items of clothing. Swimsuits were displayed on the walls, in the bow window, and wherever else space allowed. Autumn had shivered as she arranged those displays and had had to remind herself repeatedly that in some parts of the world, at that very moment, people were acquiring deep, warm tans.

Lightning broke through the distant sky and reflected in the windowpanes for a jagged instant. Autumn permitted herself a fleeting wish for sunny Florida and the Thanksgiving dinner that was by now a memory for her family. She should have gone with Ross and Lorna, she supposed, and spent the holiday at her parents' home, but she hadn't been able to face the thought of making another trip anywhere. She felt too anxious about Monday's opening, too nervous about the boutique's ultimate success, and far too restless when Cade wasn't nearby.

Her gaze drifted to the doorway connecting the store with the reception area beyond. She could see the closed door of the inner office and knew he was inside. He'd waved to her when he'd come in a little over an hour before, had called out something about catching up on his work, and had shut the door firmly. She had sighed her understanding and returned to the unnecessary last-minute cleaning.

He was waiting for her. Autumn knew that if he were doing any work at all, it would be as unnecessary as her polishing the glass counter another time. He was simply waiting and if she questioned him, he would say he didn't like her to be alone in the store. That was the truth, of course, as far as it went. But there were other elements in question. Was he still waiting for her to tire of small-town problems, the boat supply business, and the whole idea of the mini-boutique? Did he still expect her to quit at any moment and head for the nearest rainbow?

With a sigh she looked away. The dustcloth dangled, forgotten, from her fingertips as Autumn stared pensively out the window. Cade saw her that way when he opened the door. He'd intended to get a price list from the file, but purpose faded with the light that pooled around her, streaking her hair with amber. He took the few steps to the connecting doorway and leaned against the frame, watching her, wanting her.

The past weeks had been the longest he had ever known. Having her so close day after day, waiting for her to ask for his help or advice or even his opinion—and knowing that this time she wasn't going to ask—had left him restless and impatient. Why was he so uncertain with Autumn? Why did he feel he must stand in the background, watching, waiting for her to turn to him, waiting for her to know that he loved her?

The first step away from the doorway was impulsive, tentative, but with each subsequent step his decision solidified. Cade paused beside the railing that defined Autumn's corner. The boutique was on a slightly raised platform, and he rested his hands on the banister that flanked a diminutive stair.

She was very still, standing there in a wistful pose he'd seen many times before. Autumn . . . always looking out the window, seeing things he could never see, weaving dreams he couldn't comprehend. How often he'd watched her, wanting to tell her what he saw beyond that window, the dreams forming in his heart.

As she looked toward him now, his breath caught with longing and his memories fled into the faraway thunder. Her hand lifted to soothe the crumpled disarray of her hair, her lower lip tucked slightly under the upper in a sensuous, oddly self-conscious gesture, and the hesitant smile in her eyes trembled through the air to reach him.

"A thunderstorm," she said as if explaining the focus of her attention. "We don't usually have them this late in the year."

"No." His thumb stroked the glossy sheen of the rail. "It will be gone by Monday though. I've ordered clear skies for your grand opening."

"That was thoughtful." Her gaze hovered, went to the glass-topped case, returned to his. "Cade, I have a confession to make," she said with breathy reluctance. "I used my quarter interest in the company as collateral to get the line of credit from the bank." Her brows rose in wary challenge as if she expected an immediate and angry response.

"I know you did, Autumn." He watched her surprise lower that delicate arching of her brows a fraction. "Clayton called to tell me the second you left his office."

"He had no right to—" She broke off the statement to fix Cade with curious regard. "You knew, and you didn't say anything? Didn't even try to stop me?"

"I couldn't have stopped you on a bet. One way or another, you were determined to prove to me that you could handle this project. I can't say I'm thrilled with the idea, but it's done and you're committed." He paused and a smile curved slowly into place. "And I have to admit that from here, the boutique looks pretty damn good."

It took a moment before her lips parted to match the curve of his own. "Since you've made it this far, would you like an advance showing?"

He suddenly felt guilty for keeping his distance while the boutique was in progress. He had given her enough rope to fence herself in, but she'd taken it and woven a net that held him captive. His brows arched in surrender. "Are you sure you have time to show me around?"

In answer, she offered a smile and he walked up the two steps to accept. She led him from one small section of the boutique to another, talking all the while, telling him about the different clothing brands, explaining why she'd chosen one item over another, mentioning her struggle with the sun visors. The tour came to an abrupt conclusion when she moved to the display case and cocked her head to the side. "What do you think, Cade? Upper or lower shelf?"

Finally she had asked his opinion, but somehow

he lost the significance in the simple delight of teasing her just a little. "Definitely upper."

"Oh." Her mouth formed a curve of speculation. "Do you really think—" The question ended with a rueful glance over her shoulder. "Kincade O'Connor! Don't you have anything better to do than feed my insecurities?"

"Everything looks great, Autumn. You've done a beautiful job. You must know that. How can you feel insecure?"

"So easily, you probably wouldn't believe it. I've never done anything quite like this before. And it's so . . . important."

"Because of me?"

It was such a soft, undemanding question that Autumn let it drift around her before she tried to answer. What did he expect her to say? "Yes," she admitted cautiously. "Partly because of you."

He nodded as if confirming a private judgment. The storm grumbled outside. In the following silence Autumn took the dustrag and spray bottle from the counter and knelt to put them out of sight. She straightened and cast Cade a wary glance. What was he thinking? Why did he stand there looking at the boutique, at the window, at anything except her?

"You didn't have to prove yourself to me, Autumn."

She was instantly alert, her heart hesitating like a doe on the frosted edge of a meadow. Her fingertips brushed across her corduroy jeans, chafing the smooth nap. "Didn't I?" she asked. "Don't I *still* have to show you that I've grown up, Cade?"

He turned to her then, his eyes as familiar as her own, but as disturbing as the unseasonal storm outside. "No. I've been aware of it for a very long time, Autumn. It just was easier to pretend that I wasn't. As long as I could think of you as a child, I didn't have to let you go, you could always belong to me. I knew the little girl in you would continue to love me . . . but the woman?"

Autumn faced him in the momentary lull, waiting, trembling, her pulse stirring a frenetic pattern at the base of her throat.

"It hasn't been easy being your hero." His voice deepened with rough intensity. "Especially when I realized I was . . . in love with you."

Like the fragile, velvet petals of a rosebud, his words unfolded within her. Soft. Quiet. A warm, tender rush of nameless yearning held her motionless. She couldn't speak, couldn't breathe. She was melting, love flowing through her and from her as she stood, captured in his eyes, bound by her own emotion. "Cade," she whispered. "Oh, Cade."

He moved to her, lifted his palm, and placed it against her cheek. Seconds rippled past, one following another as his thumb stroked her in sensual promise. The storm rumbled closer, a rhythmic discord in a silent world. His hand left her and for an instant only his gaze caressed her. Autumn parted her lips with longing and then, in unison, she and Cade defied the distance separating them. Her hands sought shelter in his and her fingers curled trustingly into his hold. She was conscious of his strength and the power resting in his muscular body and she knew the taut, sweet ache of wanting him. And then she tasted the yielding pressure of his mouth and was lost in her need to love him.

He pulled away slowly, his kisses lingering, his hands gripping hers tightly. "Will you come home with me, Autumn?"

Yes. Her voice conceived the word, but there was no breath to support it. So she nodded once, and then again. With her fingers enclosed in his he brushed the back of his hand along her chin lightly, and he bent briefly to take her lips a second time. In unspoken accord, they turned, individually but together, making their way down the steps, leaving the boutique, walking through the empty store, getting their coats, turning out the lights, and finally stepping through the doorway into the misty gray evening.

As she waited for Cade to lock the door, Autumn turned her face to the wind and felt the first stinging drops of rain. In the time it took for him to reach her side, the storm gathered momentum and sent a wetness down on them.

"My car!" He yelled the instruction into the deluge and touched her arm to guide her, but Autumn suddenly didn't want to leave. Her eyes closed, her chin lifted, and her palms opened to the wild, pulsing beat of the rain. She was aware, wondrously aware of being alive, of loving and being loved. She was a part of this furious, pelting storm, and the storm was a viable, driving part of her. Spinning slowly around, she searched for Cade to share this feeling with him and found understanding in his eyes. Her husky laughter vibrated with the thunder and her arms rose to encircle his shoulders and draw him against her.

"I love you, Kincade O'Connor." Rain invaded her mouth and trickled down her throat. She licked the cold moisture from her lips only to find it replaced by Cade's steamy warmth. She leaned into him, feeling his body heat melt into her own desire. Lightning lit up the sky above them, but Autumn wrapped herself in his embrace and knew she had found the eye of the tempest.

Soaked through, hair sodden and plastered against her head, saturated by the icy water streaming over her, Autumn wanted to laugh aloud with the sheer joy of living. But she couldn't laugh, she couldn't shout or sing. She was breathless, drowning in his kiss, delighting in the elements of nature that whirled around her and pounded within her.

I love you. I love you. I love you. The thought was there in the rhythm of the rain, in the throbbing heartbeat of the evening. Wet, hard droplets splattered on her face and ran in rivulets to her mouth, trying to share in the tender moment of clinging lips and blending passions. The wind whipped around them, pulling at her coat and bonding corduroy to skin, twisting sleek threads of hair into tangled strands. She was cold, chillingly, stingingly cold. And yet she was content to stay where she was, in Cade's arms, in the midst of a turbulent world, in the one place she truly, finally belonged.

Thunder cracked a warning and Cade drew back. His smile enveloped her like a fleecy blanket. "I could swear I heard fireworks just now."

"And I was certain it was bells—pealing madly."

Her lips curved with a loving smile. "Let's try it again." She swayed toward him, but he caught her arm and turned her in the direction of the parking area. The full force of the wind tossed her objections to the high heavens and Autumn bent her head and let Cade half lead, half pull her to his car.

When he jerked open the door she tumbled inside, scooting across the seat as quickly as she could to make room for him. Shivering, she pushed dripping hair out of her eyes and watched as he slammed the door and turned to her with a gentle frown and a very wet shake of his head. He started to speak. Autumn saw the intention in his expression, but he stopped, the corners of his mouth tilting wryly as he held her gaze in the cool yet steamy interior of the car.

"I wouldn't trade the past few moments with you for anything," he said in a voice gentled with amusement, "but I keep wanting to say something like, 'We'll be lucky not to catch our deaths of pneumonia,' or 'Hypothermia is nothing to sneeze at.'"

Autumn laughed. She had never been so cold or so drenched or so happy. "I was thinking more along the lines of hackneyed phrases like, 'Why don't you light my fire?' or 'Let's get the hell out of here.'"

His laughter joined hers as he started the car and drove away from the store. Autumn wanted to tell him again that she loved him, she wanted to ask him a dozen things, but she was shivering now in earnest and every time she opened her mouth her teeth chattered audibly. So she settled for telling glances and warm thoughts of reaching shelter and the golden heat of the fireplace. Cade also seemed to be having difficulty in framing his words with steadiness, and the drive to his house was quiet, but fast.

Once inside, Autumn dripped onto the tiled entryway, uncertain of what to do. She frowned when she saw the long, comfortable room stretching before her. The fireplace was empty and uninviting. Even anticipating a roaring blaze offered only transitory comfort.

Cade didn't allow her much time to dwell on thoughts of the fireplace, empty or otherwise. With a brief but promising brushing of lips he helped her out of her coat and dropped it, along with his, on the couch. They didn't worry about the fact that the coats were still wet. Shoes came off next. Hers and then his. Autumn rubbed her arms and made a futile attempt at telling herself she would be warm any minute.

But not until Cade lifted her into his arms and held her snugly to his chest did she feel the tiniest glimmer of warmth. As he carried her up the stairway she nestled close to the sound of his heartbeat and was quietly grateful that he didn't expect conversation. Even if she hadn't been shaking with cold, Autumn wasn't sure she could have composed a coherent sentence. "I love you" seemed to be the sum total of her repertoire at the moment. Of course that wasn't such a bad limitation when she considered the many possibilities of that expression.

She tightened her hold as Cade pushed open a door with his shoulder and carried her inside the room. It was his bedroom and as he let her down so she stood on the carpet, Autumn remembered the one time she had tagged along up the stairs only to have this same door slammed in her face. *Come back when you're invited!* he'd told her, ruthlessly crushing her innocent wish to see his bedroom. She'd pouted for hours, but now she understood why he'd closed the door that day. To have invited her then would have invaded the moments they were about to share. His bedroom, the one room she had never seen, was the one place in his home that she entered first as a woman, as his lover.

"Get out of your clothes," he commanded before her toes had time to curl into the plush carpet. Then he was unclasping her hands from behind his neck and striding past her to the adjoining bath.

"Get out of your clothes," she mumbled, and punctuated it with a shiver. Not the most loving statement he might have said, but then again it was not the sort of comment just anyone might make. Certainly it was not worth quibbling over.

"Autumn, for Pete's sake, take off your clothes." He spoke directly behind her, his voice muffled a little by the towel he placed over her head. Rubbing briskly, he began drying her hair. She lifted numb fingers to clammy buttons and worked at separating the material, but it was slippery work and it was so hard to concentrate when he was stroking her hair over and over with the luscious soft warmth of the towel.

"I've never been in your bedroom before."

There was a slight pause in the stroking movements. "You've been here hundreds of times in my thoughts," he said quietly.

170

"Oh." A pinpoint of sadness pricked her heart at the idea. While she had been following a shadow song, Cade had been here, thinking of her. "I never knew."

There was no answer, only the faint feel of his lips against her covered head. She glanced over her shoulder, but all she could see was a draped fold in the rose-colored towel. "I like being here now, Cade."

"Autumn." He breathed encouragement along the inner curve of her ear. "You'll like being in a warm bed even better. I promise."

Her heart settled into the most pleasurable beat and she committed her attention to making progress. At last the top button of her blouse slipped free of its mooring and the garment opened slightly.

His long fingers grazed the back of her neck. A sudden whisper of desire stole her breath and she turned, her hair spilling from the towel to her shoulders. Cade faced her, his own hair glistening with moisture. A raindrop shimmered at his temple before sliding down his cheek and Autumn lifted a corner of the towel and wiped the drop away.

The velvety fabric seemed to move of its own accord beneath her hand, drying him, caressing him. A delicious tension crept through her, bringing warmth and an aching need, a need that increased as, with a seeking fingertip, he traced the open neckline of her blouse. The chill, the discomfort of wearing clothes bonded to her skin, the shivering, all fled as a tide of heat began a slow upward spiral inside her.

His eyes were deeply, intensely blue, looking

171

down into hers as he deftly flipped open the second button and the third and fourth and fifth. Her blouse peeled away with only a little resistance and fell discarded to the floor. He quickly, soothingly, coaxed her bra to follow. Then the towel slipped from her limp grasp as he pulled it around her, enveloping her in the lush velour. It swathed her back and shoulders and felt deliciously warm and dry.

With the edged hem Cade began to rub the cold from her skin. The circling massage drifted downward in a gradually slowing pattern until he reached her breasts. His gaze dropped to admire the gentle slope that seemed to lift in invitation even as he watched. His palm reached to cup and knead her breasts, although reason told him this was not the time to linger. She was cold and she was depending on him to warm her. He should have tucked her in bed, put her beneath the covers without delay, without this painful ache of wanting her past the point of reason. But she was so lovely, too tempting as she bared her breasts to him. He wanted, needed, desperately to possess her. He inhaled a long breath of control and covered her with the towel.

Autumn, however, lifted her hands to his shirt and the carefully adjusted towel slid to a tantalizing angle, the deep-rose velour underlining a deep-rose nipple. He curved his palms above her waist and bent to taste the texture of her. Slowly her fingertips inched under his collar and sidled to the nape of his neck. She held him, arching into his caress, her skin cool and damp against his tongue, her heartbeat a heated throbbing beneath his hands.

When he drew back she moved closer, not allowing the smoldering warmth within her time to abate. She worked at unfastening his shirt buttons with steady purpose, her movements supple and determined. In only moments his chest was exposed to her eyes and to the feathery quest of her fingers. Her palms rested smoothly against his chest hair as she stood on tiptoe to reach his mouth. A tiny trill of sound—low, soft—came from her throat just as he claimed the kiss she so willingly offered.

Her senses came to glowing life with the tender meeting of their lips. The scent of rain surrounded her; the taste of it was on her tongue. The feel of damp denim against damp corduroy reminded her of the driving rhythm of the storm, of the elemental passions blending in wild celebration, of the beautiful joining of lovers. She clung to him, wanting the fulfillment of her desire, yet reluctant to place even the smallest distance between them.

As if aware that the fire within was burning too quickly out of control, Cade moaned gently and created an insistent pressure at her waist. Autumn leaned back just enough to look up at him, only to find herself drawn to the fiercely compelling emotion in his eyes. Words of love, shared in silence, banked the flames to embers . . . embers that sizzled a protest through her veins.

With subdued urgency Cade proceeded to undress her. As he tugged the corduroy pants down and off her hips, he rested his lips fleetingly in the hollow of her shoulder. "What happened to the towel?" he murmured.

She tilted her head to lure him again. "Who cares?"

"I do," he responded, bending to ease the material past her thighs. "I don't want you to catch pneumonia."

"Too late." Her voice was thick with yearning. "I'm consumed with fever."

"Autumn," he said in a velvet tone that sounded oddly rough and uneven. "Please help me get you out of these wet clothes. You need to be in bed."

Yes, oh, yes. She sank onto the edge of the mattress and lifted her feet from the floor so he could pull off the rest of her clothes. Cade paused for only an instant to run his gaze over her body before he retrieved the towel from the carpet and began rubbing her feet and legs. The massage was rapid but thorough as he stimulated a pulsating heat to the surface of her skin. From toe to calf to thigh he worked, neglecting not a single inch.

Autumn watched, wondering how he could be so patient when she was trembling with impatience. Was his hunger less than hers? Did she need him so much more than he needed her? She shivered at the thought and Cade immediately straightened to jerk back the bedcovers and pull them around her. And with the fugitive frown that creased his forehead, she knew his restraint was born of concern.

Instead of lying down, as he obviously expected her to do, she caught his muscled forearms and tugged him toward her. "Would you stop trying to protect me from pneumonia?" she asked shakily.

"I'm not cold and I'm not getting into this bed without you."

His smile was a slow, tender curve. "Autumn, I'm not a martyr. I have every intention of getting into bed with you, just as soon as you let go of my arms."

Her lips formed a soft O of understanding and her fingers slipped to the tousled sheet. She drew her legs up and wrapped the bedcovers around her ankles. Then she propped her chin on her knees and watched Cade shed his clothes. Unabashedly she admired him and wondered at the anxious tension in her response. She wanted him. She loved him. And he loved her. Yet she was nervous—nervous because of her changing role in his life. Could she be the woman he needed? Could she be to him the supportive, understanding mate that he would be to her?

As he came to the edge of the bed Autumn lifted her gaze slowly, hesitantly, from his naked body to the naked desire in his eyes. He bent toward her and she opened her arms without reservation. Yes. She could be friend, lover, mate. Whatever this strong, sensitive man needed from her she would give freely, lovingly, always.

Her lashes swept languidly to her cheek as he placed a kiss at the corner of her mouth. It was an evanescent touch, gone in an instant, only to come again on the other side. Her tongue glistened a moist path across her lips, leaving them parted and trembling with his nearness, but Cade seemed in no hurry to still the light tremor. He continued the sweet seduction as with arms braced on either side of her he pressed her persuasively down to the pillow.

She followed his guidance, sliding onto the sheets, stretching her legs back and over to make room for him beside her. The raspy texture of his calf grazed her thigh in scintillating massage. The provocative gliding of his tongue along the contours of her mouth stirred the smoldering embers of her yearning. The coolness of her skin joined with his and then began to dissipate like a morning mist in the rising sun.

Cade covered her with kisses, from the subtle arch of her eyebrow to the curve of her chin, down to the aching hollow of her throat, along her shoulders and the fullness of her breasts. With each tender touch Autumn melted deeper into love. She was drifting in the ebb and flow of sensation, drawing him with her into stormy passion and gossamer delight. Loving Cade was as exhilarating as skimming the crest of the ocean waves. And with the same skill he used to guide the sailboat, he brought her whispered longings to desperate pleas.

She stroked him in turn, commanding his response by the sensuous exploration of her fingertips. For every sensitive place on her body that he aroused to fiery splendor, she found and evoked a corresponding reaction. The exquisite torture sailed on and on, until the air was thick with desire, until her heart beat against her ribs in a silent cry for fulfillment.

His mouth at her breast, his hand cupping her moist, inner warmth, Cade continued to caress her. His kisses consumed her like flames on a wintry night. Like the slow awakening of spring he stirred her senses to new life, opening her body to intimate acceptance of his. The searing beauty of their union enveloped her in the torrid heat of summer, a summer that seemed to go on forever. Then in a brilliant burst of wonder, the seasons of her life came full circle and Autumn cried out in surrender, her restless spirit winging home . . . to Cade.

CHAPTER TEN

Lovingly curled up next to Cade, Autumn teased the relaxed curve of his lips by running her finger over his mouth. He caught her fingertip with his teeth and nipped it gently. "I love you," she whispered, and he released her finger with a contented sigh.

"You have no idea how long I've wanted to say that to you."

She traced the angle of his chin. "Why didn't you?"

"It sounds so simple, doesn't it? But nothing has ever been simple where you're concerned. From the very first day you bounced onto the boat-house dock, talking every step of the way with all of your little-girl enthusiasm, you've complicated my life. It's been one challenge after another trying to be your friend, counselor, confidant, and shoulder to cry on."

He rubbed the length of her arm, his hand ruffling the contours of the sheet. "I've never really understood why I felt I had to be everything you expected . . . and more. Maybe it was because no one else believed in me as fiercely as you did." His pause was soft with memories. "No one else needed me or loved me or depended on me in quite the same way. You were special, Autumn, from the very beginning."

"Special?" She tapped his chest lightly. "You might at least have told me that before."

"Before what? You've always known you could wrap my heart around your finger."

A melancholy smile tipped her lips for a moment. She had known; she just hadn't realized what a fragile thing a heart could be. She moved to kiss him in belated apology. "I'll admit I never thought anything could change your feelings for me . . . until the day I came home and you mentioned Marilynda."

"Marilynda." The name still rolled lyrically from his tongue, but it no longer sounded secret or special. "I wanted you to think I was interested in her. I wanted to be interested in her, but even before you returned I knew nothing like that was going to happen. Marilynda and I met at the wrong time to be any more than friends. It's too soon after her husband's death for her and for me it was too late the minute I saw you standing on the dock, looking so elegantly out of place. I didn't believe you'd come back, Autumn. Ever."

"I had to look for my life, Cade. It took a long time before I realized that home is where I really wanted to be. And it took even longer to realize why. When I thought you'd found someone else, I knew you were the reason for my restlessness; you were the reason I came back."

"Richard." Cade said the name as if it were the key that solved a mystery. "You said just enough about him to make me believe you'd come home to patch a broken heart. The day he appeared on the doorstep of the shop, it was a toss-up as to whether I should shake his hand before or after I decked him flat out on the pavement."

Autumn couldn't help the laugh that winged past her lips. "Oh, I'm so glad you thought better of the idea. Richard can be such a baby about bruises."

"You sound as if you know."

At the hint of stiffness in his voice, she raised her head and leaned against her palm. Cade was not quite smiling, although he wasn't exactly frowning either. She bent forward and let him taste the reassurance of her lips. With a soft touch his arms encircled her more fully, insisting that she stay. The more subtle insistence of his mouth beneath hers was beautifully persuasive and she thought she'd never known anything as achingly sweet as loving him. The kiss became hungry, gentled, then crescendoed again before Autumn pulled away with a low, throaty hum.

She looked into his eyes and saw a remnant of question still there. "Cade, I never loved Richard. I only loved the idea of loving him."

Against her breasts she felt the vibrating deepness of the breath he drew. "Are you sure?"

"Of course. How can you even ask?"

"So much has happened to you, Autumn. Things I know nothing of. You left Eastport behind on your way to some far-off destiny. You left your family and you left me. I accepted that. I knew I couldn't tell you I was in love with you and not ask you to stay. And I loved you too much to ask that." His head moved against the pillow and he resumed the pensive massage of her shoulders and back. "On a purely selfish level, I suppose I knew you would leave no matter what I said. So I wished you good luck and told myself I'd soon forget you'd ever meant anything more to me than a precocious child who thought I was a real-life hero."

Autumn watched him, loving him as he tried to frame his thoughts and feelings into understanding.

"And then," he continued in a voice husky with remembrance, "all of a sudden you were home, full of new plans and new dreams. You were different, mature, self-assured, and determined to challenge me, to force me to see you in a new role. I didn't know how to react. For all I could tell, you'd come home with a heart in need of repair and I was the bandage that would hold your world together. It had happened before and I had to consider the possibility that it was happening again. But I wasn't strong enough to resist taking advantage of the situation. Not this time. When I made love to you that night on the boat, I was sure I'd shattered your illusions . . . and a few of my own."

Her heart heard the uncertainty hidden in his words and interpreted the hesitancy she felt in him. Dawning comprehension grew into a knot of emotion in her throat. The doubts, the reservations she

181

had sensed in him ever since that night, suddenly shifted into a pattern of clarity. The problem wasn't that Cade perceived her as a child. It was in the way he saw her perception of him. He had always been everything she needed him to be, and more. He'd been her hero and he was afraid of being less than that to her.

Her fingers whispered against the hair on his chest as she wondered how to explain that she didn't need a hero anymore. She couldn't say that to him, not when a part of her would always see him in that special, innocent way. And how could she tell him she realized he was an ordinary man with needs of his own when nothing about Cade could ever be ordinary?

"I love you," she said, hoping he would know all the emotions, all the memories, all the dreams borne by the words.

He lifted a hand to stroke her hair, her forehead, her cheek. "And I love you, Autumn. So much that it frightens me a little. I know you so well, and yet I'm not sure I know you at all."

The phone rang, a shrill intrusion, and Autumn looked to the bedside table with a discouraging frown, but Cade had the receiver to his ear before she had time to say Let it ring. With a soft resentful sigh she laid her head on his chest and listened to the deep vibrations of his voice. Although he continued caressing her hair, she was aware of the exact instant his attention was drawn away from her.

"Yes, you're probably right." His tone conveyed a reluctant resignation. "Yes, well, I'll take care of it." He replaced the telephone receiver with a clatter and tightened his arm around Autumn for a moment before he began moving away from her. "The alarm's been set off at the store. It's probably because of the storm, but I'll have to go down and check it out."

"But, Cade . . ." She didn't know what she intended to say or why she felt apprehensive. She watched him enter the walk-in closet and waited for him to come back to her side.

"You know how easily that can happen, Autumn." He tossed a shirt onto the bed and pulled on a pair of jeans. "And you know I have to go."

Yes, she knew. The accidental setting off of that alarm had never meant any great catastrophe in the past. There was no reason to worry now, simply because she didn't want him to leave. "I'll fix something to eat while you're gone," she offered with a smile. "I might even start a fire."

His grin was slow as he leaned over the bed to kiss her. "Make sure it's in the fireplace, okay?"

"You certainly have no daring spirit of adventure."

"Leaving you, looking as beautiful as you look right now, is damn daring, if you ask me."

"Then let the alarm go to blazes," she suggested.

"And who would take care of protecting *your* one-fourth of the store?" He finished buttoning the shirt as he teased her. "It's a dirty job, but someone has to do it."

"Well, please do it quickly then." She tried not to look wistful as he put on his shoes and started toward the door. "And promise you won't do anything heroic."

183

He stopped with a low chuckle, turned, and came back to her. "I can't promise that, Autumn. Right now I think it will take an act of heroism to save that damned alarm from being smashed to smithereens." His lips claimed her answering smile for a too-brief moment. "Hmmm," he murmured. "Save my place."

Then he was striding from the room, confident and purposeful, and Autumn missed him long before she heard the closing of the downstairs door. She sat for a while in the middle of his bed with the rumpled covers gathered around her. Her gaze traveled the room, savoring the knowledge that she belonged in it.

With a sense of discovery she noticed the dozens of intimate details that made this room distinctly his. A partially opened drawer with one sock half in and half out. The hairbrush, the bottle of cologne, the softball trophy, the picture of her—a snapshot taken on the day before she'd left for New York and the coveted job with Mrs. Colburn. Autumn left the bed to investigate it from a better perspective. The frame felt cool in her hand and the girl who laughed up at her looked happy and carefree, excited and just a bit uncertain. And so very, very young.

Autumn didn't understand why that made her vaguely sad, but she dispelled the feeling by walking into Cade's closet and slipping into one of his shirts. It enveloped her in warm, flannel folds and she smiled with the purely feminine pleasure that came from wearing his shirt.

As she gathered their damp clothing from the floor and started for the doorway, she cast a glance at the girl in the photograph. As soon as she could manage, Autumn decided, she would put another snapshot on his dresser. One that would give a clearer image of the woman who loved him. Maybe someday in the not too distant future there would be other snapshots of herself and Cade. And perhaps one day snapshots of a son or a daughter . . . or both.

With an irrepressible bubble of laughter Autumn wrapped herself in the magic of such thoughts. She hummed assorted melodies of domestic content-ment as she put the clothes—his and hers together, what a perfectly wonderful combination—into the dryer. She prepared a simple meal, set the table with candles and crystal, and built a blazing fire in the fireplace. By the time everything was ready she was glancing at the clock, listening for the sound of the car through the persistent beat of the rain out-side.

When at last he came through the front door the fire had died to a few worried flames. Autumn stood, hands clasped, while he removed his coat. A quick perusal revealed a tired expression in his eyes and another set of wet clothing. Without asking even one of the questions she wanted to ask, she retrieved the shirt and jeans she'd dried earlier and brought them to him. Cade smiled a thank-you, said everything was fine at the store, that he'd be right back, and went upstairs to change.

Autumn busied herself with fueling the fire and wondering why it had taken so long to shut off the alarm. Sinking onto the sofa, she clasped a pillow in her arms and waited for Cade.

"I love you." His endearment feathered across her neck and she turned her head to meet his lips. He tasted of wind and rain and she drew the coolness into herself and warmed him with the tempting play of her tongue against his. Cade moved so that he could be next to her, and his arms came about her in a tight, tender embrace as Autumn melted into his kiss. She felt his tension and knew in that moment that he needed her. When he put a small distance between them, she smiled into his eyes and tucked her hand in his.

"The storm caused the alarm to malfunction," he said without preamble, "but it was a good thing that I went to the store. There's flooding, Autumn. I don't know yet what blocked the outside drain, but the stockroom's standing in water."

"Well, at least everything in the stockroom is kept off—" The thought broke as she realized that the shipment of spring and summer merchandise for the boutique had arrived the day before and been placed on the floor.

"Oh, Cade. All the—"

"I'm sorry, Autumn. I moved them as quickly as I could, got things out of the boxes, but there's quite a bit of water damage. You'll have to sort it out tomorrow. I don't know how this is going to affect Monday's opening, but I don't think it will—" His fingers closed resolutely around hers and he drew a deep breath. "God, I'm so sorry, Autumn. I did everything I could."

"I know that, Cade." She swallowed her anxious thoughts in the face of his genuine distress. After all, even if the whole shipment were ruined, the storm

186

had shared an intangible, but wildly beautiful moment in her life. How could she worry about losing some of the stock when she possessed Cade's love? She couldn't. "Maybe it won't be all that bad. It could turn out to be a simple matter of replacing the damaged merchandise." She lifted her shoulders in a shrug of resolution. "If necessary, I'll simply start over from the beginning."

"You're staying then?"

It was a quiet statement of relief, and Autumn swung her surprised look to his face. "Did you think for one second that I wouldn't?"

His brows formed a line of self-defense. "It's crossed my mind more than once in the past couple of hours. I kept thinking about how you used to stand in the store staring out the window as if you couldn't bear being trapped inside. This afternoon I saw you with that same wistful look in your eyes, Autumn. If you had any plans to leave, the flooding today makes as good an excuse as any."

"Cade," she whispered in disbelief. "You're serious, aren't you?" He didn't answer, but she knew he was. "How could I leave now? Now, when I've finally found what it means to be home? When I've found you."

His hand came to her cheek in a yearning caress, but still she saw the hesitancy in his eyes. The doubts, the concern for her, as if in some way he were responsible for her disappointment. And with a rush of tenderness Autumn knew he had resumed the role he thought she expected. "I'm not leaving, Cade. No matter what happens, I'm staying here with you. For always. I love you. You're going to have to accept that I am grown-up now. I know the difference between adoring you as a child and loving you as a woman. I don't need you to save me from life's disappointments. I don't want a hero who can move mountains or sail around the stars. I want you. I need you to share my dreams and my disappointments and I want you to need me in the same way."

Her eyes were sincere and rich with the color of truth. Cade felt his love for her strain against the careful boundaries and self-imposed rules he'd observed for so long. She was saying words he'd wanted to hear, promising him a future for which he'd been afraid to hope. He leaned down to accept her kiss and the new relationship she offered. As she responded with such sweetness to his touch, he knew his love for her would change and grow with the changing seasons, bringing new discoveries to blend with the rich knowledge of their past.

Autumn felt the understanding, the sharing promise, in his kiss and she nestled into the shelter of his arms. *Welcome home, Autumn,* her heart sang. *At long last, welcome home.*

LOOK FOR NEXT MONTH'S
CANDLELIGHT ECSTASY ROMANCES®:

All-new

Candlelight Newsletter

**An exceptional,
free offer awaits readers
of Dell's incomparable Candlelight Ecstasy and Supreme Romances.**

Subscribe to our all-new CANDLELIGHT NEWSLETTER and you will receive—at absolutely no cost to you—exciting, exclusive information about today's finest romance novels and novelists. You'll be part of a select group to receive sneak previews of upcoming Candlelight Romances, well in advance of publication.

You'll also go behind the scenes to "meet" our Ecstasy and Supreme authors, learning firsthand where they get their ideas and how they made it to the top. News of author appearances and events will be detailed, as well. And contributions from the Candlelight editor will give you the inside scoop on how she makes her decisions about what to publish—and how _you_ can try your hand at writing an Ecstasy or Supreme.

You'll find all this and more in Dell's CANDLELIGHT NEWSLETTER. And best of all, _it costs you nothing_. That's right! It's Dell's way of thanking our loyal Candlelight readers and of adding another dimension to your reading enjoyment.

Just fill out the coupon below, return it to us, and look forward to receiving the first of many CANDLELIGHT NEWSLETTERS—overflowing with the kind of excitement that only enhances our romances!

Dell | **DELL READERS SERVICE – Dept. B428A
P.O. BOX 1000, PINE BROOK, N.J. 07058**

Name_____

Address_____

City_____

State_____ Zip_____

Candlelight Ecstasy Romances™

$1.95 each

At your local bookstore or use this handy coupon for ordering:

**DELL READERS SERVICE – Dept. B428B
P.O. BOX 1000, PINE BROOK, N.J. 07058**

Please send me the above title(s). I am enclosing $_____ (please add 75¢ per copy to cover postage and handling.) Send check or money order—no cash or CODs. Please allow 3-4 weeks for shipment.

Ms./Mrs./Mr_____

Address_____

City/State_____ Zip_____